Laughing In The Dark

*Keep laughing, sweet friend.
Love,
Susan*

Susan Swartz

Published by Open Books

Copyright © 2019 by Susan Swartz

All rights reserved. No part of this book may be reproduced, scanned, or distributed in any printed or electronic form without permission except in the case of brief quotations embodied in critical articles and reviews.

Interior design by Siva Ram Maganti

Cover images © Blink 2 Click shutterstock.com/g/Blink+2+Click

ISBN-13: 978-1948598187

*For my big sister, Nancy, who knows how
to light up even the darkest corner.*

Chapter One

As Franny drove north on the freeway, she saw three hot air balloons suspended in the late summer sky, their circus colors playing against the brown hills. She waved and shouted out, "Hello, up there." How delicious to float high above your everyday world. But then, of course, you could fall out of the balloon's basket. Or what if you decided to jump?

She raked her hand through her chopped red hair and took a big breath. Franny was terrified of high places. She'd peered inside the basket of a hot air balloon that was sitting on the ground at a fair, thinking that maybe if the basket came up high enough on her chest she might give it a try. She could always crouch down and peek over the edge. Maybe if she were with someone who would hold her in his strong, hairy arms she could stand up straight and bravely look out and *ooh* and *aah*. But there weren't any strong hairy prospects. Besides, she knew the real dread was that rather than accidentally tumbling out of the balloon's basket she might feel moved to leap out.

It was a spooky notion but she'd tried it out on others she knew who were afraid of high places and they agreed. The fear was not so much that you would clumsily trip when you got to the rim of the Grand Canyon or that you would suddenly blow a tire on the cliff side of Big Sur. Those would be accidents. The fear was that you'd have this compulsion to take a header.

Just thinking about it now made her hands start to sweat, but her mind kept going on. If she knew her life was going to soon be over, say if she had some unfixable disease but not so bad that she couldn't still get in and out of a balloon basket, maybe then she might book herself a ride. Then, if she ended up taking a swan dive over the Russian River, she could tell herself on the way down that she was going to die anyway and hers would make an interesting obituary. One way to get her name in print.

"Oh, shut up, Franny," she told herself, turning up the radio, and looking at her frowning face in the rearview mirror. She should be thinking happy thoughts. Her horoscope was working and she had three days off with her best friends. They would be sleeping on solid ground. She'd be as close to the earth as possible.

The morning was already warm and she could see last night's lopsided moon fading in the western sky. Another good omen. Tonight, if the fog stayed away, there would be a full moon over their tent. Easier to see when you got up in the middle of the night to pee and worried about stepping on soft, wiggling creatures.

She turned off the freeway and into the Dry Creek Valley, onto a winding road that would take her up into the hills and then down to Lake Sonoma. These fields, once decorated with prune orchards, were now mostly all grape vines. A glamorous upgrade for the region leading to its growing fame as Wine Country. New vineyards seemed to be filling every bare spot of the valley, but the plain hills that stood behind them were constant. Summer hills, dry as toast. No, no, how about cracked and gnarly as a baked potato.

Franny liked to challenge her writing students to come up with a metaphor for the changing Sonoma landscape with each season. "Soft and round like a teddy bear's belly," a back-to-school middle-aged mother had come up with to describe the summer hills, challenged last semester by a skinny big-eyed punk, who had shown little promise until writing, "Scruffy and tobacco-colored like a sweater from the Goodwill."

Tobacco in the summer and Irish green in the winter, the Sonoma hills were round and full, like a large-flanked woman lying on her side. That was Franny's personal favorite. Mature and female, like us, Franny thought and smiled. An astrologer friend claimed that from a certain vantage point looking down on its hills and valleys, the terrain of Sonoma County formed the shape of a uterus. If Franny ever got up in a balloon she would check to see if the astrologer was having a feminist fantasy or actually knew what she was talking about.

Suddenly there was the turnoff to Lake Sonoma and the marina. On weekends there would be a line of RVs to wait behind but today, in the middle of the week, Franny saw a straight shot down the last hill to the teal-colored water, glistening and waiting. The marina was lined with moored boats but all was quiet on the lake. And no sign of Jude's red Honda in the parking lot. This was surprising. Jude, who Franny thought looked like the brainy writer Margaret Atwood, with her intense eyes and frizzy grey hair, was always the first to arrive whenever they met. It seemed to be a point of pride with Jude, her punctuality. She would go on about, "I'm always on time. Can't stand to be late."

But, aha, today Franny was first. She drove straight down to the empty dock to unload her gear so she'd be ready when Anna, the other in their threesome, arrived with the boat. She hauled out a cooler, sleeping bag, pillow, two grocery bags and duffel. Jude was bringing her big tent for all of them. Franny laughed at her pile of indulgent excess, dug into her cooler for a diet Coke and ripped open a bag of onion flavored sun chips. Her favorite vacation junk food.

Jude knew she was running late but was on the phone with her daughter, Katy, who was teasing her about what she called her hippie getaway. "Now, Mom, remember it's not safe to get stoned and go swimming."

Jude laughed. "Katy, I'm the mother. I know the rules. Besides, we do more than party. You should come with us sometime. We actually have serious discussions. And we do so much reading. I'm bringing two *New Yorkers* and a novel I just discovered at the library."

"Which one?"

"Sue Miller. *The Senator's Wife*."

"Didn't you read that in your book club a while ago? I remember you telling me I needed to read her. "

"I did? Oh well, I'll just read it again."

"Well, don't drop it in the water," said Kate. "And, Mother? How many bottles of wine?"

"Two or three," said Jude. Actually five.

Jude enjoyed her daughter thinking she and her friends were wild and wicked. She imagined Katy hanging up and telling others in her office that her mom was off with her tripper friends. Jude would never have suspected her own mother of having too much fun, except for the afternoon gin and canasta parties with the neighbor women. Jude's mother seldom sprung herself from the house on any outing unless she was with Jude's father. People would have thought their marriage was in trouble if they went places without each other. Her mother would never have gone off with her friends to get stoned and skinny dip.

Fifteen minutes late. God. She'd felt so scattered all morning. She'd started out twice only to turn the car around, once to get her hat which she finally found in the garage and another to make sure the gas stove was off.

"Come on, brain," she said, taking a deep breath. It was just that she was excited to be going on their annual campout. It had been her idea, when? Must have been 15 years ago. "Let's leave the men and the jobs and go to the beach and get drunk," she proposed to her three closest friends. Anna, Franny and Martha.

The first year she chose Bodega Bay where the summer wind and fog forced them to spend most of their time in a soggy tent drinking brandy and playing Hearts. Jude promised to find them some place that would feel like a proper hot August. Lake Sonoma was it, inland and protected from the coast's summer furies by two mountain ridges.

She felt a little bit guilty enjoying the lake so much. She'd been part of the protest group that fought the Army Corps of Engineers' plan to dam the creeks that ran into the Russian River for flood control, water supply and recreation. It was a long nasty battle between the hippie/environmental factions and the bureaucrats and business. Everyone always expected the latter would win but Jude still regretted the sacrifice of pristine, once holy Indian land to tourism, although it did afford uninhibited women a spot to bob in the water without freezing their asses off.

Now here was the lake in all its glory and Franny waiting for her. Jude honked and waved. My God, Franny looked fabulous, in her green leather hiking boots and red shorts, like some long-legged nature goddess. Rabid about fitness and diet, she liked to say, "Either move your ass or watch it grow." Whatever happened to the rule that all women over 50 gain weight and turn into their mothers. Franny sure as hell hadn't. Of course, Franny didn't have any kids and was 10 years younger than Jude. And, of course, Franny was obsessed with eating perfectly. But now there she was, munching on a bag of chips. Not fair.

Her father had described Jude as big-boned when she was growing up. Jude later learned the term zaftig and used that on herself. She had spent decades on and off diets and once had gotten down to a size 10, but starving made her mean and she gave up. After she poured the last liquid breakfast food down the sink, she decreed the end to diets. No matter how much weight she lost and gained and lost again she was never going to look like Julia Roberts. Besides, Charlie called her pink and luscious "like a ripe peach."

"Where have you been? I was starting to worry," said Franny, hugging Jude. "You're always here before me."

"Just took a while getting started. Sorry. No need to worry," said Jude, reaching out to run her fingers through Franny's shorn red curls. No more long brown ponytail.

"You've got new hair. Cute."

"I had to do something. My kids already think I'm an old lady and the gray hair just ambushed me his summer. I decided to give myself a fresh start before the semester begins." Franny taught at the community college. Most of her "kids" were teenagers and young adults along with empty nesters going back to school and retirees.

"Oh Franny, you'll always look like a kid to me," said Jude. She knew Franny liked hearing that. She enjoyed being the relatively young one among her older friends.

"This is what we call gray, sweetheart," said Jude, pointing to her silver frizz as the two pulled Jude's supplies from her trunk.

"Hey, did you see those balloons over the valley driving up?" asked Franny. "My horoscope today said to look for good omens."

"I didn't see any balloons but a deer ran in front of me up at the bend," said Jude. "Maybe that was my omen. Not sure if it's good or bad. Scared me to death suddenly jumping out from the bushes. But she was one graceful beauty. I don't know why people around here get so down on deer. I think they're gorgeous."

"I think it depends on how far out you live in the country and how much you like your roses."

"Okay, they're pests, but in Sebastopol we usually have more complaints about gophers. Charlie says the reason people are seeing so many deer this year is because it's dry and they're looking for something to eat."

"The lake does look different, even lower this year than last," said Franny, studying the flat water, as shiny as the bottom of a pan. Sometimes the lake had a kind of alien look. It looked like what it was, something created not by nature but by bulldozers and men with hardhats and clipboards. The shoreline was raw and some of the remaining trees stood in water up to their knees, bleached reminders of the once dense chaparral of scrub oak and Manzanita.

Jude was from Michigan which was blessed, she liked to say with "real authentic lakes." But it was also full of bugs, which Lake Sonoma was not. Up here if you had a boat you could find some wonderful warm water, private swimming holes and wilderness camp sites without mosquitoes. To get there, they needed Anna.

Anna and her husband Rick owned a small boat that they moored at the lake. It used to be Rick's fishing boat until he upgraded to a bigger, faster model. For many years he and Anna had taken their son and his friends out on the boat, but it was pretty much Anna's now. She'd changed the name, ignoring Rick's protests about that being bad luck. She re-christened it *Lucia*, after her late mother, and painted it canary yellow.

Right now, *Lucia* was in a bitchy mood, which was often her way. There was always something a little unpredictable about *Lucia*, which added to their annual camping adventure. One summer they had to be towed to the marina by three burly boaters with Russian accents who came to their aid when she stalled out in the middle of the lake and refused to budge. Anna was embarrassed to finally ask for help but her friends thought it was great fun to be rescued by a group of Russians who kept asking, "Where are your boys?" as if the reason for their predicament was that they'd lost their men and Boris and his buddies would be happy to fill in. Franny had spent a lot of time thanking the men for hauling them back to the dock, going below for "a couple of shots of vodka in the interest of world harmony," she said. After that, any time *Lucia* refused to do their bidding, Jude would sing out, "Oh Boris, where are you?" and wink at Franny.

Anna had been getting to know the boat better. She couldn't leave it to Rick to come running with his tools every time *Lucia* pitched a fit. She took time this morning checking the oil and extra gas can and gave the boat extra minutes to warm up. She poured the last coffee from her thermos and reminded herself this was her vacation, too. Her friends could wait on her. Their only responsibility for the annual trip was to get themselves up to the lake. She'd been here for more than an hour, cleaning the boat, making room for all their gear.

Still, she was proud to be her own skipper. She liked the idea of women and boats, particularly old women and their boats. One of Anna's favorite movie scenes was in *Julia* when Jane Fonda, as the wise and weathered Lilly, sits alone in her fishing boat on a lake, staring into the gray morning. It's the last scene in the movie. Everyone good in Lilly's life is gone but she's got her boat and another dawn. Maybe that's how it would be for Anna someday—an independent woman with an old hat on her old head in trusty old *Lucia* if the tug made it that long.

"Here comes Anna and *Lucia*, shouted Jude as the boat rounded the marina and aimed for the dock. In the buttery daylight *Lucia's* yellow hull looked like a big bobbing toy waiting for them to climb aboard and play. Jude and Franny quickly stowed their ragtag gear on board. You could tell all of their family camping days had been a while back, thought Anna. Jude's Sears' tent was a model no longer made which is why she couldn't get a replacement pole for the one that was missing and caused the tent to sag at one end. "I'm sentimental and I'm cheap," said Jude, when asked why she didn't get a new tent. Anna's flannel sleeping bag had been Robby's, decorated with cowboys and ponies. Franny, on the other hand, liked having the latest gear, including a solar powered radio with a charger even though cell service at the lake was sketchy.

Jude had to admit that while Lake Sonoma might not be as big and woodsy as a Michigan lake it felt like the best place in the world to be on this late summer day, heading down the wide middle to reach the smaller inlets and their favorite spot at the west end of the lake, past the jet ski zone, past the beach overrun by church groups, remote enough they could strip down and bake sunny side up if they felt like it.

Jude liked the whole scene—Anna steering with a cup of coffee and looking slightly intense and Franny hanging over the side to get mist in her face like a dog out a car window. Jude wished for it, for them, to never change.

They came around a bend and chugged down a creek to camp site, number 12, unclaimed and waiting for them.

"Hurray, it's ours," said Anna. "But what happened here? Look how big the beach has grown," she said, cutting the engine and drifting to a much broader shore than usual.

"Look how far up the old tree is," said Franny, pointing to a bare leafless tree which normally stood in the water where they could tie up *Lucia*.

"Welcome to the drought," she said.

"Welcome to Wine Country where there's more wine than water because the grape growers suck it all up," added Jude.

"And the wannabe mansion owners grab the rest for their Hollywood lawns," chimed in Anna.

Getting angry at environmental spoilers was one thing the friends had in common although they weren't exactly back-to-the-landers. Their old friend Martha had described them as "middle class imports from someplace else who came to Sonoma County because we wanted to live next to nature but were relieved to find a Macy's."

They unloaded in their usual manner. Franny set up the beach chairs, threw her book on one and scampered to help Jude set up the tent on a flat spot of what might have been grass earlier in the season but was now scuffed dirt with a few weeds. Anna secured the boat. They did their work quietly like good Girl Scouts, knowing the reward. Sweaty from their effort, Jude opened her cooler. "Beer here."

The late afternoon sun was fierce and the hot dry grass spiced the still air. From her siesta spot under the boat's awning, Franny picked up another aroma and watched Anna rolling a joint. She packed it leisurely, and after lighting and inhaling deeply held it out towards them.

"Actually, I think we're going to have to start blaming some of this water problem on our second biggest crop," said Anna. "Pot farming takes a lot of water."

"I don't think anyone's growing here, at the lake, do you, Anna?" said Franny.

"Who knows? They're growing it everywhere. This little tasty came from our book club farmer friend in Freestone. Shall we?"

Franny grabbed the joint. She really shouldn't, she thought to herself. Pot tended to make her a little paranoid. But it was a once-a-year indulgence. The others were more into it. Jude and Anna liked to talk about getting stoned and going wild at concerts in Golden Gate Park. Anna often said that being at the lake made her feel that same freedom, "like when we were pretending to be hippies, dancing around half naked. Of course, it helps if you're high."

But Franny had seen enough kids with drug problems at school. Still, once a summer with her lovely friends in this dreamy oasis she allowed herself to indulge in a nice safe buzz of daytime stoniness. Stripping off her T-shirt and shorts, Franny slipped over the side of the boat, welcoming the lake's light, tangy smell and kicking past the weedy banks into the soft, cool depths. Flipping on her back, she stared up at the hills, imagining what critters were up there looking back.

Deer would be up there, whole families, maybe even the doe Jude saw this morning. Wild turkeys, too, more of them every year, and bobcats, supposedly. One year they saw hoof prints that Jude swore were from wild pigs.

Snakes, too, but Franny wouldn't think about them. She was a big baby about snakes which is why she would high step when she walked the dirt trail up the hill to where county parks had inconveniently located two outhouses.

Snakes aside, Franny worried more about people. Ever since the killing of three women at Yosemite by a psychopath she replayed how something like that could happen here, to the three of them. She tortured herself with how that would be. A man would suddenly come off one of the wilderness trails and hail them like a friendly hiker. He would be chatty and decent looking and he'd start asking about their boat and one of them, probably the ever-trusting Jude, would offer him a beer. Then just as they were all relaxed he'd pull out a gun and grab one of them and drag her up the trail and the rest would be too panicked or stoned to know what to do. It made her sick and scared to have these kinds of thoughts, which is exactly why she shouldn't smoke pot. And now Anna had gone and mentioned pot farmers. Maybe they were up in the hills, guarding their crop with guns. One more thing to worry about.

She headed back to the boat, feeling suddenly cold and no longer enjoying her nakedness. There was a splash and then the grinning face of Anna. "Hey, what were you looking for up there?"

Franny thought of saying, "Just some mad man who is trying to figure out which one of us he's going to rape and kill" but instead said, "Maybe the ghosts of old native mamas enjoying us liberated hussies."

CHAPTER TWO

ANNA WAS ONE OF those women who becomes handsome with age, thought Franny. Without her glasses and with her wet thick hair slicked back, you could see those high cheekbones and almost inky eyes. Some smile lines. Anna had a generous grin and good teeth.

"How's your sweet husband?" Franny asked. "I saw Rick at the deli downtown last week and we waved. My friend from work said, 'Who's that?' and I said, he's taken. Rick is so cute. I don't think he looks any different from when I first met you guys."

"He's good old Rick," said Anna, "but right now I'm pissed at him."

"Why? Is it still about his mother wanting to move to California?"

"Yes. Ever since Rick's dad died, she's been hinting that she's ready to leave Pennsylvania and be closer to us. And didn't we have extra space now with Robby gone?"

"Oh, you mean actually move in with you guys? That's big."

"Yeah. Big. Too big."

"She's pretty elegant, as I recall," said Franny, "although I only met her once when she and your father-in-law came out that Christmas."

"Elegant, yes. And judgmental. And demanding. And Rick goes along with her every wish."

"Well, you know they say you can tell how a man will treat his wife by how he treats his mother," said Franny, climbing up the ladder and swinging her tanned legs into the boat.

"Yes," said Anna. "But if both are living in the same house, I think I know who will get the better treatment."

Jude was in the boat and going through her cooler. "Shit. Where is the damn cilantro? Did anyone bring any extra cilantro? How can I make guacamole without cilantro?"

Franny opened her cooler and waved a leafy handful under Jude's nose. "Ta-dah."

"Ooh," said Jude, backing away. "I really don't like the smell but I do love the taste. I thought I brought some. I know I went to the store for it yesterday."

There wasn't much of a galley on *Lucia* except for a tiny propane stove with a miniature oven. Jude, who'd volunteered to do the first meal, went to work on cheese quesadillas to go with her guacamole and a cabbage salad.

"Anyone ready for wine?" she asked, holding up a bottle of sauvignon blanc. By the time dinner was ready another white had replaced the first along with a red. "We do eat well," said Franny, dipping her finger into the last of the guacamole and topping off their plastic wine glasses. She and Jude started cleaning up the galley and Anna went to the stern to look at the darkening sky.

She looked around at them and asked, "Do you think Martha's looking down at us tonight?"

Martha, part of their original group, had died in a freeway crash in Los Angeles seven years ago. She was the most kick-ass of the bunch, her friends agreed. An adventurer with many lovers, no children, brave and lusty, the first to announce she'd found, "oh my God, the first gray pussy hair."

She died when she 53. Martha did not live long enough to see one of her old boyfriends elected to the state senate, watch her rented bungalow in an orchard leveled to make room for grapes or to get old with her friends.

Martha's death hit them like scared children. At her memorial the three friends stood together silently, hoping for someone to clap their hands and announce it wasn't real and have Martha reappear.

Martha's car was rammed by a panicked teenager who was running from the highway patrol. How ironic that fearless Martha, who thrilled to white water rapids, hiked to the tops of volcanoes and took off by herself on a bus through Ecuador after reading a book on rainforests, would die in so common a spot as the 405 on a Friday night.

Jude once dreamed that she saw Martha in a passing subway car. Jude yelled out "Martha" and Martha acted like she heard her, then smiled and turned away. Jude felt snubbed, like she'd been closed out of a conversation at a party. They all had been such tight friends even though Franny knew Martha first. They had met in college and Martha eventually followed Franny to California, connecting immediately with Anna and Jude.

Now Jude walked over to Anna and they clinked glasses. Anna started humming a favorite Martha song and broke into, "Come on. Come on. Come on," and they all wailed, "Take it. Take another little piece of my heart now baby."

Franny waved her arms in the air and hopped around until Anna shushed them. "We'll be scaring the coyotes."

They sat quiet until Anna said, "Do you think they allow Janis Joplin music in heaven?"

"Sure. Janis got up there long before Martha. They probably became good friends," said Franny.

They stood quietly and then Jude said, "If there is a heaven. What if you die and the music just stops?"

Ignoring her, Franny said, "Can't you see Martha walking in to this big room full of people and they all stop talking and stare at her, kind of part the crowd for her to walk through, because she's the new one. And then the music starts and it's really good music, not just angel harp tunes and Martha starts swinging her hips and waving her arms."

"I think if heaven is a dance scene it's more like something out of the *Nutcracker* with the Rose Queen greeting everyone," said Anna.

"Not if you always hated ballet when you were alive," said Franny, now wishing they could change the subject. She chewed on a fingernail and started to worry about dying. What bothered her the most was not what happened after you die, but doing the dying. The in between of now you're here and now you're not. The awful dark and lonely transition.

Franny thought again about the Yosemite women. It happened many years ago but Franny remembered every grisly account of the murders of the mother, her daughter and her daughter's friend. They must have been frozen with fear, no time to run, call for help, or grab for a lamp and crack the crazy guy's skull. No time to rewind the tape and decide instead to have an early lunch and drive home from Yosemite a day early.

And Martha, did she see that jerk in her rearview mirror and try to get out of his way? Was she afraid at the last moment? Did she think, "that idiot is going to hit me." Or was she thinking ahead to the plate of mussels she could expense at some fancy restaurant?

The CHP said Martha died instantly but what does that mean? One minute you're thinking whoa, there's a guy coming towards me much too fast and what an asshole and then…nothing.? A blast of white? Everything smashed and loud and then nothing. The other driver, the one trying to outrun the cops, also died on impact. Did he and Martha look at each other as they were leaving their bodies and say, "That was stupid."

Franny wondered if religious people know these things better. Did any priest or rabbi know anything more than the part leading up to dying? Maybe she should start going to church. She could try the Unitarians. A friend from the junior college had invited her to join her Unitarian dream circle. But Unitarians seemed so "whatever" about everything, including, she suspected, how it all ends.

Franny's uncle—mean as they come, racist, crummy to his kids, no particular reason for him to be on the planet—that creep died with his mouth open, asleep on the couch. Kind, wonderful people like Martha don't get to die like that. Nor did Franny's father who struggled to breathe his last months, gulping oxygen, barely able to swallow. Who lets an Uncle George be carried off after one last Bud Lite and Franny's father hang on in torment?

Franny felt tears coming. They always talked about Martha when they got together at the lake. There was always one toast to Martha, and Franny imagined Martha stopping by to join them.

But why all this talk about dying, or was this an inevitable subject as you get older?

Franny looked over at Anna staring into her glass of cognac. This must be getting too much for her, too. Anna had gone through breast cancer. Franny supposed that dying was more real to Anna. She remembered when Anna told them about the lump in her breast and how scared they all felt. Martha was still alive then. Everybody still felt young. They hadn't thought much about one of themselves dying. Anna had been a champ, insisting from the beginning she would beat it but for a while that's all they talked about whenever any of them got together. How was Anna doing now? She seldom talked about it anymore.

Anna had been so brave, said her breasts had served her well, fed her baby and that Rick would be okay. "Rick's more of a leg man anyway."

Back then is when Anna had started smoking a lot of pot. She told Franny and Jude, "It keeps me calm, especially when I wake up in the middle of the night and think, oh that's right, I have cancer."

Franny looked away and said, "I think I'll get into my sleeping bag and read."

"Let's go," said Anna. "You coming, Jude?"

"No, I think I'll sit here a while and watch for shooting stars."

Jude knew it would be a long time before she could sleep and if she went inside the tent they'd keep talking and Jude needed a break. She sat in a beach chair and smoked one of the Marlboros she'd smuggled in. She preferred tobacco to pot. Smoking calmed her, which was different from when she had been younger and cigarettes gave her jittery energy. There were so few people to bum a real smoke from these days. It was such an antisocial act in California, she wouldn't be surprised if some camper downwind might right now be twitching his nose and looking for a ranger to file a complaint.

What a funny place her adopted state had turned into. People getting all lathered up over other people's smoke, perfume, seatbelts, processed foods, trying to entice the ants out of the house rather than kill them. The other day Jude had asked for ant poison at the new market in Sebastopol and the clerk looked at her like she'd ask for bomb making materials. Most of the time she didn't notice how much she, too, had slipped into the PC mode. Then, someone from out of town would visit like her cousin Betty, a no-nonsense New Jersey cop who Jude took wine tasting. They had gone into a Dry Creek Valley tasting room and Betty started to pull out her cigarettes as if she were in some Jersey saloon. Jude grabbed Betty's arm and practically dragged her outside and told her she couldn't smoke inside a tasting room. Betty rolled her eyes but went into the garden, only to be admonished by a fussy young man who ordered her to move to the far end of the parking lot "if you really must do that."

"Forget them," Betty told Jude. "I'll buy their precious grape juice at my liquor store back home where I can smoke where I want."

All this worry about smoking, Jude thought. Something's going to kill you. It might as well be something that you enjoy. Jude had long stopped worrying about the personal hazards of smoking, at least to herself, although she was glad Katy didn't smoke and she'd be nagging Charlie if he still smoked cigars. A lot of Jude's clients smoked. Who could blame them, beaten up by life and their husbands? Sometimes Jude joined them.

"Jude, are you out there smoking?" said Franny from the tent.

"Who? Me?" Jude said.

She stared at the lake. The moon was so bright it looked like someone had left the stage lights on their little cove and switched the rest of the world to black. The moon turned the trees in the water to marble sculptures. Jude wondered how long those poor trees, left standing when their meadows and woods turned into a lake, would continue to hang on. Another summer they might all be gone, knocked over in a winter storm if they ever got one again. Maybe they'd just grow tired of pretending to look alive. A few years ago, people all over Northern California had started losing their oaks to sudden oak disease. The experts said it was related to what caused the potato famine in Ireland. Jude and Charlie, like nervous parents, regularly examined the oaks in their downtown park, checking for leaves starting to turn white and bark getting scaly as if they had dermatitis.

Their campsite tree was as smooth as a telephone pole. It looked like it had been nuked and was long past worrying about something wanting to kill it. Beautiful thing though, like a Georgia O'Keefe piece.

Geez. How could she get so hung up on a tree? Her brain sometimes took off on the wildest detours. Jude closed her eyes and put her face up to the moon. She used to tell Katy that a moon bath brought good luck and magic. Jude hoped that were true.

Quiet conversation continued from the tent. Jude was happy to be separate from the chatter. Too much talk sometimes hurt her head. She felt the same way at home. Some nights she needed to get rid of the noise and would take a cup of tea and slip out on the deck to sit for a long time wrapped in her robe. She might forget to come inside if Charlie didn't shout out the bedroom window, "Where's my lover girl?"

Last week Jude forgot something else. She'd come home from work, walked into the living room and sat down, putting her head back. She must have been there in the fading light for an hour. The house was empty. Charlie was at a meeting. A ringing phone cut into her consciousness but she decided not to answer and let it go to voicemail. When she checked the voice said, "Jude, it's me." The puzzling thing was that Jude recognized the voice, but couldn't think of the name or the face to go with it. This sometimes knowing and not knowing worried her. She squeezed her eyes tight to make the name come but it didn't. The voice sighed and said, "Okay. Sorry to miss you. But we'll talk at lunch tomorrow."

If that were all, Jude might have turned the incident into a funny story to tell Franny and Anna. "So, not only could I not name my mystery caller, I could also not figure out my mystery lunch date." Then one of the others might say, "Oh, that's happened to me before" and tell about a similar time when she, too, blanked. Then Jude could relax because forgetting was normal. Senior moments, Charlie called them. Anna called them brain farts. Jude didn't think either one was amusing.

She rationalized that she never had that great a memory. She had trouble in grade school memorizing the poems she and her class were supposed to recite for gold star stickers. For years she'd been saying that name tags should be mandated by law. She always had to look up how long to cook corn on the cob. And lately, with the added clients at the shelter, how could anyone be expected to remember all the names you had to keep in your head.

The night of the mysterious phone call she finally thought to look in her day planner to see who she was meeting tomorrow.

Jesus, it was Linda. Noon, Toscana's. She'd known Linda longer than she knew Anna. It was unacceptable for her to not know the voice was Linda's.

But that hadn't been all that happened that night. When she got up to find her planner, she saw the full grocery bag on the chair next to her and it was oozing chocolate ice cream across the blue striped upholstery. This was bad. She'd forgotten the goddamned ice cream.

No, Jude wouldn't tell that story. Nobody would think that leaving a half gallon of ice cream on a chair was brain fart funny. She'd cleaned the mess up before Charlie got home.

Tonight's sky was enormous and packed with stars. Jude looked up and mouthed the word "Orion."

Bingo. No hesitation there. Her brain was clicking now. She would report tomorrow morning that she had seen an amazing… an amazing…What do you call it? Shit. Not a galaxy. Dammit. Come pretty word, tell me your name. Constellation. Yes, that was it. Constellation. Constellation.

None of their group ever swam after dark, not even Franny, but Jude imagined herself standing up and walking slowly into the lake, following the moon path, regal and assured like Mary Queen of Scots walking to the executioner. She'd have to keep her flip-flops on because the bottom could be rocky and she didn't want to stumble. She'd want to glide into the water, barely making a ripple, as silent as a cormorant. And then could she keep walking until the lake took her? It probably wouldn't be that easy to put your head under water and slowly sink with dignity. Who was it who had drowned herself with rocks in her pocket? The moody writer with the big eyes and long nose. Think, Jude.

CHAPTER THREE

ANNA FIRED UP THE stove for coffee, wound her long hair into a top knot and reached for her glasses to watch Franny emerge from the tent. Franny squinted at the sun just starting to squeeze over the yellow hills and waved. Their pajama party scene was not strong on fashion, but Franny was easily the best dressed, wearing purple pajamas, in what was no doubt fine grade cotton. It was probably a good investment for single women to spend good money on attractive nightwear, in case they got lucky, thought Anna, looking down at her own plaid nightgown and green sweatpants. That was one of the perks of long-time marriage, that you didn't have to spend much money or time dressing for bed. It had been years since Anna slept in anything matching or color coordinated.

"Jude's still asleep," said Franny, pumping some pink cream from a bottle and rubbing it on her face. She offered it to Anna and said, "Have you noticed how many creams you use on your face and body when you get older? I have four basic moisturizers. My mother had only one."

"Ponds," said Anna and Franny together.

Franny pursed her lips and mimicked the singsong style of a makeup clerk. "First, Madam, we have the renewal cream for your face, then cellulite smoother for the thighs which is also quite nice on the derriere. May I also suggest a dab of progesterone cream for the neck, only $180 an ounce. And this new miracle moisturizer from Italy."

"Hah. What they don't tell you is that you're never going to have skin like an Italian unless you were born Italian."

"Actually, I read somewhere that Asians have the best skin," said Franny. "From all that fish oil and green tea."

"I think it's more genetics, but whoever you are, it's crazy. We're not supposed to worry about getting older but we're all buying this anti-aging stuff. Rick kids me about all my potions," said Anna, passing the bottle back to Franny. "Maybe it is foolish to keep oiling this aging body. But it makes me feel like I'm still trying. You know?"

"Absolutely," said Franny, opening a tube of lip balm. "My granny would spend an hour fixing herself up, putting on earrings, perfume and lipstick even after she was pretty much housebound. My mom would kid her about being vain, ask her if she was trying to vamp the UPS guy. But it was for herself. Granny liked looking and smelling good. I would watch her study her face in the mirror. She was still smiling at herself at 92."

"That's like Rick's mother," said Anna. "That woman always has her face on."

"Then, good," teased Franny. "Maybe you two can play make-up when you're living together."

"Oh dear," groaned Anna, crossing two fingers in a hex sign.

Jude lay on top of her sleeping bag in the musty tent, the dusty canvas starting to bake in the morning sun. She could hear Anna and Franny laughing on the boat, probably drinking coffee which Jude sorely needed. But first she had to try to piece last night together. Could she even remember going to bed? What was she so worked up about? Did she dream about drowning? That made her think of one of her favorite old movies, *Coming Home*. Bruce Dern returns from Vietnam and is all messed up from the war and finds out that his wife, Jane Fonda, is not only a braless peacenik but having an affair with Jon Voight, a paraplegic vet. Bruce walks right into the ocean and disappears.

Jude wondered if she would have the guts to do something like that if things started to go terribly wrong. But how would she know? Did her mother ever know, for sure, what dark narrow tunnel she was heading into?

The first signs, at least the ones Jude picked up on, were when her mother, Ruth, started sounding vague on the phone, almost like she didn't want to talk. When Jude had asked what was wrong, she said, "Nothing. I'm just tired." By the time Jude could take off from work to fly to Michigan to check on her mother, Jude's father was dying. All efforts went toward him, the fierce lawyer who drank too much and had a heart attack. His sudden collapse, which he survived for a month, undid everyone so Jude's mother's odd behavior didn't stand out as all that inappropriate. At least not at first.

Jude and her sister Patsy watched their mother sit at the bedside of her dying husband and quiz him about the dry cleaning. "Where is your brown suit, David? Did you pick it up? You should let me be in charge of what goes to the cleaners. Is it with your winter things?" Jude's father said nothing. Jude widened her eyes at Patsy and shrugged her shoulders.

Her mother moved through the funeral guests as if she were entertaining the relatives at Christmas. Cheerful even, directing Jude and her sister to get food and drink for everyone. And smiling, standing at the casket, looking down at Jude's father and making comments, saying how nice he looked in his Brookes Brothers'.

Jude saw one of the women from her mother's church talking quietly to the minister. Jude thought she heard the word Alzheimer's and was pretty sure her mother did too, because Ruth suddenly appeared frightened. Back at their parents' home Patsy got out their father's Scotch, poured three glasses and patted the couch for her mother to sit. "Mom, how are you doing?"

Ruth started to fidget, twisting her handkerchief and Jude said, "Can we do anything for you?" Ruth stood up and shouted, "Stop it. Just stop it." Later Jude found her mother in the kitchen staring out the window. Jude went to put her arms around her and Ruth said, "Please Jude. I don't want to hear anything bad."

Oh God, thought Jude. She'd die if that was starting to happen to her. But that was the problem with Alzheimer's. You don't get to hurry up and die from it.

Franny hollered, "Hey Jude. Hey Judee, Judee, Jude. Rise and shine. We're drinking all your coffee."

Okay, Jude thought, these are my friends. They love me. If they thought that I was getting a little too dingy, Franny or Anna would say something. Wouldn't they? She needed to stop scaring herself. Maybe she just had some tiny benign brain tumor.

As Jude squeezed in at the table, Franny passed her a bagel and said, "Anna was asking if I was still dating Jack. The answer is no. He was always flirting with younger women. Like, we were at the Buena Vista in North Beach, a sparkling night in the city and I'm feeling pretty sexy. Skinny black jeans and my purple boots. Jack had a new phone and was asking me to pose. Then he stands up and walks past me to the next table to take a picture of two women seated behind us. Young, blonde, with tight little shirts that showed their bellies.

"They giggle and I turn around to smile in a good-natured way as if to acknowledge that he's harmless but go ahead, indulge him. I can't tell if they're flirting back or laughing over this funny old guy. Jack, of course, is beaming like he is every woman's gift and I'm thinking it's pretty pathetic that it takes three women to feed one man's ego."

Anna groaned. "When Rick and I were in Paris a few years ago, up on Montmartre where they have all those artists in front of their easels, one of them waved at Rick and asked, 'A portrait of the lady, monsieur?' Rick shook his head no and the guy said, "Mustn't wait.' I sulked all day because I thought he meant, man to man, 'Time's a-wasting.'"

"Well, did the guy do your painting?" Franny asked.

"No way. I looked 100 years old that morning," laughed Anna.

"Well, I feel like 100 years old this morning," said Jude, taking off her robe and wading naked into the lake.

From across the water they could hear motorboat sounds heading their way. Franny jumped up and shouted, "Boat" to Jude who was floating on a plastic raft. Jude flopped into the water as a blue speedboat rounded the curve and came up their creek.

"Hey, this is a no-wake zone," shouted Franny. "Slow down." The boaters waved back as if she'd called out a friendly greeting but didn't slow. As the driver did a sharp U-turn away from them,

Franny noticed two small children inside and yelled, "Get some life preservers on those kids."

"Dopes," said Anna.

"Stupid," said Jude, heaving herself back onto the float.

There was no agenda for their second day although they would usually take the boat to one of their favorite swimming holes for a late afternoon cocktail swim. Before they did Franny said she needed a hike, grabbing her water bottle and sticking a notebook in her pocket.

"I'm going to read," said Jude. No matter what her daughter Katy said, Jude could not remember this Sue Miller. Nothing in the story seemed that familiar. Maybe she should hike, too. Good for the brain. But she couldn't keep up with Franny's strong legs.

At the gym one day, someone had asked Jude if Franny was her daughter. Jude laughed but it hurt her feelings. Franny wasn't that much younger. Okay 10 years. Jude could have whispered. "Don't be fooled. That's not her real hair color, she bleaches her teeth and she's had work on her eyes."

Franny had convinced her eye doctor that her eyelids had gotten a little saggy and made it difficult to put in her contacts. "I kind of exaggerated, so the insurance would cover it as a medical need," she told Jude. "I felt a little guilty until I read that Gloria Steinem had hers done and decided if it's okay for Gloria, why not for me?"

Franny came back from her walk waving a skull. "Present," she said. Jude had a collection of animal skulls planted around her garden and now here was Franny bringing her a new one while Jude was having bitchy jealous thoughts. She blew Franny a kiss and took the eyeless creature.

"What is this," asked Franny. "Cow or horse?'

"Maybe human," said Jude, caressing the head. "Alas poor Yorick. I knew him," she said, getting the smile she wanted from Franny. "Maybe some old farmer went off into the hills to die. And now you've disturbed the bones and he'll come looking for his head in the night."

Glancing at Jude's book, Franny said, "Didn't we read that in book club?"

"Oh," said Jude. "I think I missed that one."

"Hey, did you guys hear sirens? I thought I heard something when I was walking back there."

Jude shook her head. "Everything here has been utterly quiet and still, except for those yahoos in the boat earlier. But now I think it's almost cocktail time." She grabbed one of the bottles of red wine.

"Zin in the afternoon, Jude?" said Franny. "Aren't we supposed to be drinking something chilled and white?"

"It's my brain medicine," said Jude, with a short laugh. "Don't they say that about red wine? That it's good for brains."

"To keep us from getting Alzheimer's, you mean?" asked Franny, taking a pull on her water bottle.

Jude felt a sickening lurch in her stomach. "Something like that."

Anna chimed in, "No, I thought it was blueberries. Or is that for something else? Wait, maybe it's pomegranates."

"If it's wine we have nothing to fear," said Franny.

"Dark chocolate, too," said Anna.

"Again, no worries," said Franny.

Anna revved up *Lucia* and the trio aimed for a corner of the lake where the water was deep and there were flat diving rocks. It meant having to go toward the marina and cut through busy water traffic but this afternoon there were surprisingly few boats in their path.

"Where did everybody go?" Anna asked. She gave the boat full throttle and they churned toward the marina. Anna suddenly slowed and yelped as she saw a dozen boats in a semi-circle facing the dock. People were standing and looking toward shore where red lights flashed.

"Oh God, something's happened," Anna said, getting behind the cluster of boats and next to one whose driver was looking through binoculars.

"Franny, yell over and ask him what's going on," said Anna.

"He thinks a child fell in the water," reported Franny. "They're keeping all boats back while they search. Look, there's an ambulance. And a firetruck."

"There's that blue boat from this morning," said Anna. "Oh no, do you think something happened to one of those kids?" She strained to look. "I'm not sure what to do. Should we help look?"

"No, don't move. Let's wait," said Franny "Don't you have any binoculars on board, Anna?"

Anna fished a binocular case out of a side compartment and passed it to Franny. "You look."

"There are people in the water and someone bending over from the dock. Could be a person in a uniform, like a paramedic. Now looks like they're diving in. I can't tell. Maybe they found something," said Franny. "Oh God. It looks like someone holding a body."

"Jesus, let me see," said Anna, pulling the binoculars from Franny's eyes.

Just then they heard a shout from the closer boat. "They've got her. They've got the kid." And then there was another shout, "They're doing CPR." And after that a series of shouts relayed from boat to boat to the last happy report. "She's crying. She's breathing."

"Thank God," said Anna, feeling tears begin and turning to hug Franny and Jude who were also crying. Anna took a deep breath and blew it out. "Well, now I guess we just leave." This was like drivers coming across a crumpled car on the freeway marked by flares and emergency vehicles, gaping at a tragedy and moving on, grateful it wasn't them.

"This is so weird," said Jude. "Just last night I was thinking about how it would be to drown." Her friends seemed to be paying no attention but Jude went on. "Once when I was little, we were at Lake Michigan and they brought the body of a boy to the beach. The lifeguard worked on him but he was blue. It gave my grandmother the chance to lecture us all about never going in the water without a buddy. I stared at that kid's blue face until someone covered him up. It stayed in my head for a long time. And then last night I..."

"Jude, please, can we hold off on the drowning stories," said Anna. "So, what shall we do? Do you guys want to go back to camp or to the swimming hole? We're pretty close if you want to swim."

"Swim, I guess," said Franny.

Anna motored to the rocky outcropping and threw out an anchor. "Okay, nobody go in until I turn everything off."

Jude stared into the water. "Remember that old movie with

Shelly Winters and Montgomery Clift where he rows her out into the lake and she suddenly realizes that he wants to kill her?"

"Yeah," said Franny. "Because he fell in love with Elizabeth Taylor. But he doesn't get away with it. They never get away with it."

"I think," said Jude, "that in movies you're not allowed to get away with it. At least not the old movies. But I bet plenty of people do. How about that movie at Lake Tahoe where the mother sinks the body of her son's gay lover? She got away with it."

Franny looked over at Anna who was shaking her head and crying. "Why are you two talking about movies?" said Anna, wiping her face. "That child back on the dock could have died. She almost did. That's how things happen. You start out on a sunny day at the lake and then everything changes. You turn away for a moment and your child disappears. Can you imagine the panic they felt when they knew that little girl was overboard? My God, you'd be out of your mind."

She could hear the panic in her voice but couldn't let it go. "When Robby was three, I lost him at the mall. He was suddenly not there. I don't know if I dropped his hand. He was just simply gone. I couldn't believe it. I became this crazy, hysterical woman. I lost it. I kept yelling his name and asking people if they saw a little boy in a Mickey Mouse shirt. I was practically insane when a security cop suddenly came walking up with him, holding his hand."

She started to cry again and Franny put her arm around her. "Honey, Robby's fine. What is he now? In his 30s?"

"32," said Anna. "But just like that, everything can be over. Poof. Those damn parents, or whoever they were, should have had life jackets on the kids. This can be a big scary lake. Anything can happen."

"Let's just go, Anna," said Franny. "I don't much feel like being in the water right now. Let's go back to camp and make dinner."

They sat around the table until a cool breeze had them digging in their bags for sweatshirts. When the sun went down Anna lit candles while they wiped up Franny's Greek salad with pieces of bread. "My own tomatoes and cukes," she boasted. Jude added a bowl of pesto pasta, saying, "My own basil."

"Have you ever noticed how women never feel like we should take the last bite?" said Franny, looking at the last chunks of feta and Kalamata olives at the bottom of the bowl. "We could sit here for another hour and munch and there still would be one little bit of food left at the end of the night. Men are different. They will take the last piece of pizza and have it jammed in their mouth before they think to look up and ask, 'Oh, did you want some?'"

"Well, let's break that rule right now," said Anna, scooping up cheese and olives and popping them in her mouth. "From here on I say, take it while you can. And now for dessert," she said, bringing out a chocolate mousse cake, bottle of port and opening her silver box. "My own medical marijuana."

CHAPTER FOUR

EVERYTHING WAS STILL. NOT even the water felt like moving, thought Franny. Really, it was amazing how quiet life could get at the lake, everything smoothed over, even a child's near-drowning, boats hushed, no phones, no wayward squawk of music sneaking into their cove from another campsite. On their second night they all seemed to want to hold on to their last free time together, like little kids gorging on the end of summer. This was the best way to camp, thought Franny who had once tried a meditation retreat.

"It was a Buddhist boot camp," she'd reported. "Two whole days of silence. We couldn't even talk while we were making dinner. Or eating it. Or putting on lipstick in the ladies' room. I get enough of that living alone."

Their raucous bliss-seeking Lake Sonoma style was better, she declared, toasting naked in the sun, getting drunk under the moon and talking long into the night. By this time tomorrow night, Franny thought, she'd be back in her empty house, already missing her friends. She dotted the cake crumbs with a wet finger, put them in her mouth and said, "If you could do one thing different in your life what would it be?" That was a subject that should keep them up a while longer.

Anna looked up and straightened her glasses. "Is this an interview question, Franny?" she teased. Franny was their interrogator. All those journalism classes.

They stashed their dirty plates in the galley sink and left the boat, bringing wine bottles and glasses to shore and lining up their chairs by the tent. Franny lit a lantern, propped it against a rock and continued.

"I just mean do you ever wish you could make an abrupt career turn? Or move to another country? Be with a different man? Okay, maybe not you who have such fine adoring husbands. But do something bold? Have an adventure?" She looked expectantly towards Jude who was usually willing to bare her soul. But Jude, her arms folded across her chest and slunk back in her chair, was quiet.

Jude nodded her head towards Franny. "You say first."

"I would like to write a book that becomes a movie so I would know I don't have to teach at the junior college forever. I would like to meet someone who I want to live with until I die and not be alone. I wish I had been braver younger."

"Brave enough to do what, Franny?" asked Jude.

"Brave enough to say 'yes' to chance. Be like your Katy is, Jude. Take off for the city not knowing a soul, study Italian, get a tattoo, hang out with sculptors and intellectuals."

"Does my daughter do all that?" Jude asked, feigning surprise.

"I know she has an owl inked in black above the crack in her butt," said Franny, "because she showed it to me at your Christmas party. Katy seems so worldly, confident. I envy that. She also still has opportunity to have excitement in her life. I feel like I've given up on that. By my age I should have had more lovers and written something edgy that shocked my friends and got me in the *New York Times* Book Review." She took a breath. "Well, maybe not a whole review, at least a mention in the New and Noteworthy Paperbacks."

No one interrupted, so Franny continued. "Or if not, gone the more traditional route. Live in the suburbs, have a bunch of kids and complain about being a stressed-out soccer mom. Instead I have, what? A little bungalow in a cutesy-pie town with no single men. And I'm teaching other people's children how to write their memoirs before they're 30 and who, according to what I read, are having more fun than I ever did."

Anna was only half-listening to Franny. It was not a new theme. They played the "what if" game a lot when they were together. Anna suspected that in Franny's case it was often an invitation to get enough strokes to help her conclude that her life was just fine, enviable even. Everyone needed validation.

"Franny, are you really that unhappy? You know you're a great teacher. You told me at the end of last semester your department head gave you a superior evaluation. And we're always telling you to please write the book, which you, if any of us, has the time to do."

Before Franny could protest, Anna kept on. "You do have the time. You're single. You get the whole summer off. And, if you'd wanted a bunch of kids you could have had them when you were married to Tim. But he bored you."

Franny grimaced. "I thought I'd jumped too soon into marriage and might be happier with someone else. That's my point. When you're younger you have a lot of choices. You don't have to settle. But I did settle. Pretty soon I'll be 58 and things will be dull for the rest of my life. And, as I've reminded you before, Anna, teachers do not get the whole summer off."

Anna could have reminded Franny that she found her first lump in her fifties, and that was her big life adventure. But instead she said, "I've always told you, Franny, your life sounds pretty sweet. When Robby was still at home and Rick was in one of his black moods, I often thought about you in your clean and neat little Victorian. I imagined you listening to classical music and taking long baths surrounded by candles, while at my house it was chaos and tension and sticky bathroom floors. You'd talk about popping down to the plaza and having dinner at some hot new café I never heard of, and I wanted to be you."

"Hmm. Did you also envy me sleeping with a dog and talking to my plants?"

Anna hooted. Sometimes Franny was so self-absorbed, probably from being single and having no one else to worry about. But her talk of regrets reminded Anna of something. "I know about those lost youth moments. I had one when Rick and I were staying over in the city. We passed a boutique on Union Street and there was a single poppy red dress hanging in the window. The wall behind it was that Italian gold color and that scene set up the most incredible longing in me. I stared at it like it was a painting in a museum that I wished I could be part of. The dress was slinky and cut low and probably cost a fortune and, come on, realistically where would I ever wear such a thing. But it made me feel like I'd missed out on something, that I should have included a red dress in my life."

Jude jumped in. "You can put me in a red dress when I die. A red dress might be a nice finish," Jude said, fluffing her corkscrew hair and smiling broadly. "Remember, I told you I got married in a red pantsuit, mostly to defy my mother who said large women should avoid bright colors. I could go out the same way. I think I'll tell Kate. Bury me in red. And you guys will have to do my makeup. And make sure the jewelry doesn't look too coordinated, like it came in a set. Make me look stylish, so that people will look down at me and say, 'I never realized Jude was so elegant.' The creep who worked on my mother made her look like a Kabuki doll. And that woman was one proud classy Brit. She would have been horrified to see herself. That's one reason we told them to close the casket."

"Actually, Jude, I'd rather have the red dress while I'm still alive," said Anna. "When I die, I want to wear my jeans and a black turtleneck. Because if I'm going to spend eternity in one thing, I want something comfortable, something basic."

"That's true. Jeans do go with everything," Franny giggled. "But what if heaven isn't California casual and they expect you to dress up?"

She stood, stretched and yawned and poured more wine into their glasses. "Uh oh, we've veered into our new favorite subject. And wait until you hear this. A woman at school has her very own casket sitting in her living room. She uses it as a storage chest and coffee table. It has extra blankets and pillows inside and, on the top, a pile of magazines and candlesticks. But one day she'll be inside."

"Now that is ghoulish," said Anna.

"I think it's kind of nice," said Jude. "When our old neighbor died her kids laid her out in the living room in a cardboard box. It was a nice box, painted green with flowers. Then they drove it and her to the crematorium."

Anna groaned and Franny said, "Just think of the savings in funeral costs."

"Actually, I want my ashes to go in a fancy urn like that hippie artist out at the river makes," said Jude.

"You just said you wanted to be buried in a red dress," said Franny.

"Oh, that's right," said Jude.

"But if you did want an urn you could buy yourself one, Jude, and use it as a vase," said Franny. "Sweet peas for now. Jude, later. What would your New Jersey cousin think of that? Wine Country dying."

Jude stopped laughing.

"Jude, it's a joke," said Franny. "Come on."

Jude picked through the wine bottles, looking for one not entirely drained. Turning back to her friends she said, "Okay, since we're on the subject, I wonder if any of us would be brave enough to help a friend die? Just curious."

Anna gasped and Franny stared at Jude.

"What do you mean, Jude?" said Anna. "Like that Dr. Kevorkian? Is that what you're talking about? Didn't he go to prison for helping people die?"

Jude nodded. "Well, I guess he's not available. I just wonder if someone you knew, someone you loved, was very sick and wanted to die but it looked like it was going to take a very long time, would you help her?"

"Do you mean get her some pills or a gun or something?" asked Franny. "Isn't that a crime, like being an accessory?" This was a weird, crazy-ass turn. What did Jude mean? Was this wine talk? Could they maybe go back to Anna envying Franny's life?

Anna stubbed out her joint and said, "There was a story when I was growing up about a well-known doctor, actually he taught at the med school, who was married to a woman with MS and they agreed that when she became really bad he'd help her die. He had all the pills stored in the house that she would need, and one day he went off to work and left her with the pills. I think she mixed them into some pudding. She was dead when he came home. What was creepy about it was that it sounded like he got her all set up and left her. Like he said 'Toodles' and drove off to the office."

"Oh, come on, Anna," said Jude. "He wouldn't have said 'Toodles.'"

"I know. It's just that it bothered me that he wasn't with her. I hate the idea of suicide but I think he should have stayed. To hold her hand. To make sure it worked, at least."

"Maybe he had to stay away so that he wouldn't look like he was a co-conspirator," said Franny.

"Well, everyone, at least his friends, my parents, knew he'd helped," said Anna. "He talked about it as if he were proud he could help her."

"And if you're a doctor in a small town," Jude said, "and no one is going to make waves or even ask for an autopsy, then that might work. But most people aren't protected like that." She stood up but kept talking. "I think they were lucky. No one was going to call the coroner or ask for an investigation. Maybe she didn't want him to be there at the end. Although, I don't know who would want to be alone. I wouldn't."

Franny jumped in. "Maybe that was just a cover-up. Maybe he murdered her and made it sound like she was in on it and that he was a loving, compassionate husband to help her along."

Franny thought for a while. "I think I'd have to be very sure that person was definite about wanting to do it. And how would you ever know? A day later maybe they would have changed their mind."

"But what if it was the mind," said Jude. "What if that was the sickness, that the mind was going and someone needed to end it while they were still in their right mind. What if each day they were losing a tiny bit more of their mind? And what if suddenly the next day they lost the decision-making part?"

"Whoa, now, Jude. I'm starting to get this," said Franny. "You're talking about your mom, aren't you? I know it was rough on you and her, but do you think your mom would have really wanted to die. Or wanted you to help her die?"

Jude had asked this same question to herself many times when her mom was sick. "I don't know. I asked her once when she was in the nursing home. I whispered to her that I could help her if she wanted to go. She just looked at me with blank eyes. She could have started screaming for the nurse, 'Help, my daughter's trying to kill me.' Or maybe she was thinking to herself, 'It's about time you asked.' But she said nothing, indicated nothing and we all waited. Eventually she died on her own. Eight years it took. And she probably had it two years before we even knew."

Anna sighed. "That must have been awful, Jude. But I don't think anyone can assume that another person would prefer to die just because you would if it were you. Maybe your mom wanted to keep living."

Jude felt her face growing hot. She started to walk away and kicked an empty bottle on the ground. "Really, Anna? I do not believe that in my mother's scrambled sick brain there was one clear wish to live. I don't think she liked wearing an ugly yellow sweater that a nurse stuck on her that probably came from some dead woman down the hall. I don't think it was her choice to be trapped in a room like a POW with a babbling roommate who never turned off her fucking loud television which no one happened to notice was always on some shopping station. You don't know everything, Anna."

Anna gasped. "God, Jude, I'm sorry."

Jude felt embarrassed. She had wanted to get into this slowly. All the wine had made her go too far. She tried to back up. "No, it's okay. I'm sorry. I just don't think anyone else gets it, that there are far worse things than dying." As she said that, she felt even worse because that wasn't fair either. Especially, oh Jeez, to Anna. She made an apologetic shrug in Anna's direction and walked off. "I need to go pee."

After she left, Franny whispered to Anna, "What's going on with our friend? Why were we talking about this?"

Anna was wondering the same thing. Jude often said the worst thing that happened in her life was her mother getting Alzheimer's and had wept about her, especially when she drank. But this was more anger than grief. She sounded almost desperate and that wasn't Jude. Jude was the steady controlled one, their rock.

Franny brought the lantern into the tent and she and Anna got out their books to read when Jude opened the flap. "Sorry guys," she said. "Must have been the wine."

Chapter Five

Jude turned her head to the window flap, away from Franny and Anna. She suddenly felt so alone, even lying next to her best friends. She should be able to whisper something inane like "Nighty, night," but she was embarrassed.

And she felt so needy which was unlike her. How much could she let down and tell them? Her friends told her everything. She knew things about Franny that Anna didn't. And she'd heard confessions by Anna that she promised never to repeat. But who was her confidante? She knew she had spooked Anna and Franny tonight and she better find out if something was really wrong before she brought it up again.

Her mother never told her own close friends about her illness. Jude's father and the rest of the family didn't seem to suspect anything was seriously, catastrophically wrong although after their father died Jude and her sister wondered how much he knew and had kept to himself. Alzheimer's wasn't as much in the news back then. The film star Rita Hayworth, the beauty with the red hair—Jude's mother was a fan—was the first real big name to be connected to the disease.

"Rita Hayworth, the face of Alzheimer's," some magazine writer had labelled her after her death. What a legacy. Did that lovely face take on the blank eyes of Jude's mother? The timid smile? Today, Alzheimer's was a common scourge. People made Alzheimer's jokes when they forgot a name, couldn't find their keys. But those who actually had the disease still kept it a secret as long as they could. Of course, President Reagan got it and it didn't seem to hurt his image, seeing as how some Republicans still thought of him as a political genius.

Maybe Jude wasn't on her mother's awful path. She'd perked up last week when she read about a woman whose memory problems were thought to be caused by pesticide poisoning. Maybe Jude had been poisoned. She even called her sister Patsy to ask what their parents had used on their vegetable garden in Michigan when they were growing up.

"My God, Dad's tomatoes were huge every summer. He must have doused them with something toxic," she said to Patsy.

Didn't Patsy remember their father walking around with a pump, spraying powder on his garden every summer? "I'm sure he didn't think of it as poison," said Jude. "Back then they even believed DDT was safe."

Her sister had been no help at all. Patsy couldn't remember their dad spraying anything. She didn't even remember the tomatoes as anything special. She teased Jude that she'd become, "One of those hysterical left-coasters, blaming every ailment on someone sinister poisoning the land, when some poor farmer is just trying to make a living."

Jude teased Patsy back. "Maybe your brain isn't so hot either if you can't even remember Dad's tomatoes."

Unable to sleep, Jude unzipped her sleeping bag and felt the cool night air on her skin. Maybe she'd be okay. She'd read a newspaper story about a man who had a type of stroke that only partially affected his brain. The stroke slowed him down but the man had been able to continue quite well as an artist. He was almost cheerful in the interview, explaining that he was doing fine except for having to give up his truck and not remembering how to tango. His wife joked ha, ha, he'd never tangoed in his life.

Jude could handle not driving if that were the deal she had to make. She'd accept a mini stroke and get Charlie to drive her everywhere. They could sell her Honda. They'd need only one car and could buy something cool—maybe a silver sports car. Charlie could pick it out.

If she had something minor, maybe she could even keep working. Everyone else at the shelter acted a little flaky, which happened when you busted your ass trying to find housing and food for damaged women while the good old boys in Washington kept robbing the poor to give tax cuts to the rich. Maybe she could claim it as a work-related injury. She could get her doctor to say her brain was weakened from an overdose of pity and frustration. She could go on disability.

But Jude couldn't stand it if she had Alzheimer's because there was no lesser form of that disease and no cure. She knew that because she had a fat file of news clippings, she kept in her bottom desk drawer. She'd started collecting Alzheimer stories when her mother was in the nursing home. There were so many sad stories and no hopeful ones.

Jude knew she couldn't hide for very long if she did have it. She'd have to tell someone she was afraid of what was happening to her and at first, they would probably protest, "Oh Jude, of course you don't have Alzheimer's," but they would begin to watch her and treat her differently. Even tonight she might have said too much. What if Anna and Franny were each thinking they better alert Charlie or Katy when they got home. She had to go slow, and crap, crap, crap, be brave and probably, maybe, go talk to her doctor.

Packing up, taking down the tent and rolling up sleeping bags gave them something to do to avoid chatting. They all felt awkward. Franny yanked out the metal tent poles which clanged to the ground. She winced and grinned sheepishly at Jude. "Hurts the old cabeza, doesn't it?"

Anna took over folding up the tent. "Such a trusty old thing. Hope she lasts another year." She stuffed the tent into the boat and asked, "Does anyone want a swim before we go?"

"We always stay until after our lunch swim," said Franny.

"We can if you want, but I told Rick I'd be home by early afternoon," said Anna. That wasn't true. Rick didn't expect her until dark, might even use her coming home late to have a couple of drinks after work. She felt like it was time to pack up. Maybe it was all the death talk yesterday and Jude going on a nutter last night. She thought they all sensed the party was over.

Franny pointed to three black turkey vultures circling the

trees across from their campsite. "I hate those things. They give me the creeps."

Trying to joke, Jude looked up from rolling her sleeping bag and said, "Oh Franny, they don't want us. They're just looking for some yummy dead mice for breakfast, doing their nature thing."

Franny pushed her clothes into a bag and sighed loudly. Now she was worried about Jude and she didn't want to be worried about Jude because Jude was like a big sister. Her family was Jude's family. "Okay, no swim," she said.

Jude took a deep breath and stood up. "All right. I'm sorry I blew up last night. It was crazy. I'm not even sure what happened. I guess I drank too much. It is true, some say, that we don't hold our wine as well when we get older."

"We didn't drink all that much," said Franny, adding a small laugh. "It's okay, Jude."

"Yes, it's okay," said Anna, putting an arm around Jude. "But let's go."

They were silent on the ride back to the dock where Anna dropped Franny and Jude. They quickly hugged goodbye and Anna yelled out "Talk soon" as she aimed *Lucia* back to her slip. The lake might stay sunny and sparkling but Anna expected she would drive home into an overcast day which would fit her gray mood just perfectly. She could see fog squatting on the ridge, getting ready to swoosh down on them.

Anna wondered if Jude was simply being drunk or weird last night or was seriously troubled. If Jude really had something bad going on, Anna and Franny would become her ladies in waiting just as her friends had been for Anna.

The summer Anna found the lump she hadn't told anyone until after the campout. Maybe it was typical of women or maybe just Anna. She didn't want to ruin anyone's fun. She'd always been that way, even to making it a point to not schedule doctor appointments until after vacation. "Who wants to screw up a perfectly good trip with bad news? If it's coming it can wait until I get home."

It was after a trip with Rick to Italy that her doctor found a lump. Anna told her friends only after she'd had the lumpectomy. The cancer was in situ, relatively good news. A big warning really. They'd cut it out and she'd waited to see if she had to do chemotherapy.

Martha had been the first to pledge solidarity, swearing to shave her head if Anna lost her hair to chemo. "We'll all go bald together and put on our war paint and fuck-me shoes and march into the bar at the Hotel Healdsburg." When Anna found out she didn't need chemo Martha pretended to be disappointed. "What, no sister act?"

Cancer was not the shameful secret it had been for Anna's mother's generation. Anna had joined a support group where they talked about breast cancer openly, looked at photos of tattooed mastectomy scars, studied reconstruction techniques and shared the effects of cancer on your love life. That helped Anna stay upbeat and optimistic and she often spoke of her disease almost like it was cancer light, even though it had taken her mother, slipping unchecked into one breast, then the other and finally having its way with other organs.

Anna had small breasts, "so there's not much to lose. It's not like I'm known for my big, beautiful breasts." But she liked her breasts. They had a nice round shape and when she feared losing them, she wept. She loved having Rick touch her breasts, make circles on them with his tongue. She owed some of her best orgasms to those nipples.

She'd ended up having the breast removed after she found the second lump. "Off with it," she'd said to her doctor, sounding more cavalier than she felt. Why had the damn thing come back? She'd wake in the night and think, where else is it growing right now.

That time, to help, Franny came up with the idea to make a plaster cast of Anna's original two-breasted self the week before surgery. They invited a few other women and gathered at Franny's for sushi and then the friends covered Anna's torso with cold wet strips of paste and cloth. After the form hardened, Anna removed it and they took turns signing the inside of the cast and decorating the front. Anna had painted the marked breast, the one about to go, tomato red with a bright golden nipple covered with glitter and a shooting star coming from its center.

Now she'd grown used to her reconstructed body and had almost stopped worrying that the slightest twinge in her back or a sudden headache meant the enemy had slipped back. Next year she'd bring a cake to the lake and add a candle to mark another cancer free year.

But would there be a next time at the lake? What in the hell was up with Jude? She'd have to have a heart-to-heart with her. Maybe, first with Franny.

Since Anna was really in no rush to get home, she got off the freeway and took the back road to Petaluma, one of her favorite routes, cows on one side, grape vines on the other, now starting to bulge with purple fruit. She rolled down the windows and inhaled. "The return of the poop," she said out loud and laughed.

Every year in late summer Sonoma County would have visitors cringing as they took a whiff and looked at the bottoms of their shoes. It was the Sonoma Aroma and came from dairy farmers draining their holding ponds and spreading cow manure on their fields. The idea was to return nutrients to the soil, and on a hot day when the wind was blowing, the ripe perfume wafted through the region.

A prospective client had recently asked Anna about it. The woman was clearly a snob and someone who didn't hang around barnyards and Anna had already decided the woman would be a difficult sale and likely not worth the commission. When they walked out of a stately Petaluma Victorian the woman inhaled, gagged and asked, "Oh dear. Does it always smell like this?"

"Oh, yes, most of the time," said Anna.

It was along this road where the artist Christo installed his famous Running Fence, a gauzy white curtain dancing over dairy land and around cattle ranches to dive into the Pacific surf and flutter in the summer sunset. How those farmers had resented him back then, this effete artist with his French wife, Jeanne-Claude, seeking permission to trample over their pasture land with what the couple called installation art. What a hare-brained idea, to spend all that time putting up the thing just to take it down two weeks later. But Christo and the flame-haired Jeanne-Claude charmed the farmers and the county supervisors and the world had driven up Highway 101 to marvel at the curtain which actually marked a turning point for the region, put it on the map in a way, and helped change Sonoma County's image to something approaching hipness. Some of those distrustful farmers still kept pieces of the curtain as valued souvenirs.

Could be one of those farmers now, Anna thought, spotting a guy in jeans and plaid shirt walking toward an old white house. He was with a black dog and they moved slowly, like arthritic companions. Was there a wife inside waiting for them, making an early dinner, she might call supper, maybe some green beans and fingerling potatoes from her garden? Would she greet him with a kiss? What would the old farmer and his wife talk about while they ate?

Anna did not look forward to how life would be when she and Rick retired and were home all day together. She wasn't sure she trusted the happy talk of retired couples who insisted they were having a great time and loved not going to work. What do they do with each other all day? At least she'd always have her friends to call and say, "He's driving me nuts. Let's plan a get-away." She needed to work on Rick to get some more friends of his own before he quit working so he'd have an escape plan, too. She didn't want him watching ESPN all day.

Anna rolled into the driveway. Rick was getting out of his truck. "Hey babe," he shouted. Then she saw the green BMW. "Guess who's here? Mother."

Chapter Six

Franny thought of the Naked Lady lilies as the last pink of summer and they made her both happy and sad. Indomitable things, every summer, just when you thought the lumpish mound was ready for the compost heap, little green shoots sprang into tall stalks and pink feathery blooms popped open.

By late August, houses in Franny's part of town sported a chorus line of Naked Ladies—known by purists as Belladonna Amaryllis. The tall pink plants had probably been around since the first Healdsburg farmhouses and now rooted in front of quaint over-priced bungalows like Franny's. Their smell reminded Franny of a damply perfumed choir director she had in junior high, and she liked to describe their pinkness as "somewhere between bubblegum and Pepto Bismol," but she liked their attitude. "Standing on high heels, tossing their pink curls, saying 'yoo-hoo.'

"The only problem with the ladies," Franny said every year, "is they mean that summer is over and school will be starting."

Franny took a cup of tea to the front porch, joined by Oliver, her golden retriever. She cut a dozen Naked Ladies and set them in a bucket of water to keep on the porch. She couldn't tolerate their sugary scent inside but their bold pink stood out against her blue house with the apricot trim. She wondered what her neighbors answered when asked who lived in the house of many colors. She hoped someday they could say, "a famous author" instead of junior college English teacher.

Every year June Franny left the JC campus determined not to return. She'd have most of three months to find a better alternative to returning to her old job in September. Each year she thought maybe this would be the summer she got an advance on a novel or interested a publisher in putting together a collection of short stories.

Summers were Franny's dedicated time to write. In July she'd gone to a writing workshop in Mendocino. The year before she'd been to one in Napa. One summer she got accepted into Squaw Valley. Workshop instructors encouraged her to keep writing. Fellow students complimented her characters and humor. She was always scribbling down ideas, random thoughts and overheard dialogue in one of many notebooks, and she did get the occasional piece in a literary magazine and small press anthology. But no agent nor big publisher with big money had come along, not this year or any.

"I'm thinking I need to stop writing about adventure," she told Jude when she got her latest rejection for a novel about a medical librarian recruited by the CIA. Franny had liked it so much, she envisioned it becoming a PBS series but no one else did. "Not believable," said one of the many publishers who nixed it.

"Maybe you should write about your world, Franny," was Jude's advice. "Maybe you're trying too hard to make up stuff you don't know about."

So now here she was again. School had started and instead of waving a book contract and celebrating her retirement Franny had returned to campus, walking under the same oak trees into the same stone building, smiling hello to the same people and starting one more same year. All she had to show from the summer was a new haircut, which was at least noticed by Holly, who taught poetry. Holly had spent her summer on a bike and barge trip through France, inspiring a bunch of new poems, causing Franny to sigh with envy.

"How about your summer, Franny? Did you guys do your wild thing at the lake again?" Holly had asked. And before Franny could go into details, Holly said, "You should write about your getaways. They sound like so much fun."

Franny thought about that as Oliver flopped his big head onto her lap, nudging her hand for an ear rub. It was true. They did always have fun, but this last time something was off. There was the near-drowning of the little girl and then Jude went all crazy-ass on them. It saddened her to think about Jude but then suddenly she tapped her finger to her lips and said, "Maybe Mama has an idea, Oliver."

Franny had picked up a message from Katy after school started, asking when Franny was coming into San Francisco to meet her for lunch. "I'll take you someplace cool and Zagat-approved so you'll have to leave the clogs and jeans at home. I'm dying to see you."

In spite of their age difference, she and Jude's daughter had a strong friendship. There had been times, especially when Katy was in high school, when Franny got the call for help because Katy didn't want to call her parents. When she needed a ride home from a drinking party where she wasn't supposed to be. When she needed an excuse for cutting class. Kid things. Then there was the day Franny accompanied a trembling Katy to the Women's Health Clinic for an abortion where protesters screamed, "Don't kill your baby" and Franny looked them straight in the face and glared. Katy told Franny that she could have asked her mother to go with her but then her father would have found out and it would have been too much for Charlie to handle.

Now just into her 30s, Katy was funny and bright, a confident career woman. Franny didn't agree with her middle-aged contemporaries who said they'd never want to be young again. Franny would adore it, having a second chance to make more of her youth. Katy seemed to know where she was going in life. She had told Franny her plan was to spend two more years at the ad agency in San Francisco and then go to a bigger or different market. Maybe New York. She'd also said she hadn't yet fallen in love with anyone who was going to get in her way.

As Katy had promised the restaurant near SF MOMA was crowded with stylish professionals talking against background music that Franny wished she recognized. The maître d started to ask if she had a reservation when Franny looked over his shaved head and spotted Katy at a corner table. It was so like Katy to show up first and not appear self-conscious sitting alone. She wore a dove gray suit and palest pink shirt that managed, even with cuffs, to look alluring and showed she was well out of her Urban Outfitter phase, except for maybe the lime green rhinestone-studded sunglasses she whisked off as Franny sat down.

"You look great," Katy said to Franny.

"You too, as always," said Franny, studying Katy's face in approval, but thinking something looked different. "Do you wax your eyebrows?"

"Yes, and that's not all," said Katy and winked. How does a 30-year-old affect such worldliness, wondered Franny, who had dressed all in black and been picking Oliver hair off herself on the drive down.

They chatted about the cold summer, traffic on the bridge, downtown parking nightmares and tempted each other to try the wine-roasted oxtails. Instead, they both ordered salads, dressing on the side. At a previous lunch the subject had been thong underwear and Katy had forced Franny to Victoria's Secret to spend $20 on a tiger striped G-string that was still in her underwear drawer with the tag on.

Katy suddenly looked serious and said, "Franny, have you noticed anything wrong with Mom?"

"What do you mean, honey?" said Franny, wanting to avoid relating the weird camping night episode with Jude. "I haven't seen your mom since Lake Sonoma but we've talked briefly on the phone. What is it?"

"I don't know. I thought if anyone, you would know," said Katy, her eyes growing big and watery. "Sometimes she acts so odd, like she's off in another world or hiding something and when I ask her what's going on, she gets snappy. I can't even tease her out of it. Dad says she's just being moody and it's probably hormonal. But Mom's way past menopause."

"Maybe it's the job," said Franny. "Your mother works too hard, always has, and takes her cases to heart. Who wouldn't? She hears women every day talking about their husbands beating them up or spending all the rent money on drugs. It has to get to her. Maybe it's time she retired. She probably should have stuck with PR. No one gets that overwrought doing public relations."

Katy gave her a weak smile and pushed away her half-eaten salad. "When I was up there last, I overheard her making an appointment to see her doctor. I asked her if anything was wrong and she said, "Oh, I just want Carly to look at another skin bump. Routine thing." I asked if that was all, and she said, "Sure." But I wondered if she was being honest with me."

Franny liked looking at Katy. She had Jude's wild mane which Katy tamed back into a knot, with loose curls over her ears. Jude would be so pissed if she knew her daughter and best friend were talking about her over lunch. But the fact that Katy was concerned enough to come to Franny meant something serious might be going on with Jude.

"I guess I should tell you that we had a bit of a fight when we were at the lake, and I have been meaning to ask your mom if we could sit down and talk more about it."

"What did you fight about?"

"Truthfully, I'm not sure, Katy. Your mother is a complex person, not always easy to figure out even though she always seems so well adjusted and happy."

"Yes, she does like to put on a happy face," said Katy, motioning to the waiter to fill her water glass.

"But even so, your mother—my best friend—has got to have as many demons as the rest of us. We all want her to be solid and good ole Jude. We need her to be that way, for us. Maybe she's tired of being the rock."

Should she tell Katy about the morbid stuff, Franny wondered, stalling while she poked through the bread basket and picked out a small roll covered with sunflower seeds. She broke it in half and said, "Need to go easy. I didn't get to the gym this week," hoping Katy, also an exercise addict, would be prompted to switch topics to her latest hot workout. But Katy stared at her, wanting more.

"Okay," said Franny, "The conversation did get a little strange that last night on the lake. Your mom started crying about your grandmother and then she got into talking about how death was better than being sick. Then she got mad at me and Anna because we didn't agree with her. Really, I just didn't want us to keep talking about dying."

Katy jumped in. "That's it. She's gotten dark. I thought maybe you guys were reading too many vampire novels. Mom cracked up one night telling Dad and me what she thought was a funny story about this man at work who buried his father in the wrong cemetery in the wrong county. The guy didn't find out until after the funeral that his father had bought a plot in the cemetery in another town and been paying on it for years. Found a receipt tucked in the old man's wallet. When the family came home after burying him, they found bird shit all over the front step and this guy knew it was his father letting him know he was not amused.

"Dad and I kind of laughed but Mom busted up and then she got real serious and said that before she dies she's writing down detailed instructions. She grabbed my hand and said she'll let me know what she wants to wear and that I have to be the one to dress her."

Franny groaned. "Yeah, she told Anna and me she didn't want any orange lipstick or matching jewelry."

Chapter Seven

"Hmm, looks like a keratosis. Old sun damage, like the other ones," said Jude's doctor, after peering at the tiny brown skin bump on Jude's shoulder. "Nothing major to worry about," said Dr. Carly, putting away her magnifying glass and patting Jude on the shoulder.

"I know I come in for these a lot," said Jude, "and I blame it on my high school gym teacher. She was also the health teacher. She was great at coaching volleyball but not so much on health, except she beat us over the head with cancer warnings, especially the one about any noticeable change in a wart or mole."

"Well, that's okay. She did a good job. Did she talk about other things, like lumps in your breast?"

"Are you kidding? She was too squeamish to mention the word breasts. I think she told us to read some manual and talk to our mothers. But she was a nut for moles."

Carly looked up from writing in Jude's chart, laughed and said, "We all worry. I was in Bali last month on vacation and spent it obsessing over a mysterious pink patch that I suddenly noticed on the inside of my knee, probably because I was wearing shorts for the first time in years. The only way I could see it was to twist around and look at it with my makeup mirror. I was miserable until I got home and asked one of the other docs to take it off."

"And?"

"It was nothing, but it kind of wrecked Bali."

Jude had been Carly's patient for years, long enough to be on a first name basis and talk to her like a wise and reasonable friend. They compared menopause stories, even though Carly was at least 10 years younger. When Jude complained of insomnia Carly prescribed the sleeping pills she used. They shared the same acupuncturist for headaches.

"Let me go get the liquid nitrogen and we'll zap this and you'll be done," said Carly. "Unless there's something more, Jude."

This was her moment, to either thank Carly, give a hug and leave, or speak up. The skin appointment had been her excuse to get a chance to talk to her doctor, to tell her that what bothered her was much more than a benign subcutaneous annoyance to be frozen away. And wouldn't it be wonderful if Carly could wave her frozen wand and burn into Jude's brain and fix what was messing up her precious neurons?

She took a breath and said, "Well yes, Carly, there is."

Jude knew there was no way to tell conclusively if someone has Alzheimer's. Her mother's doctor had told Jude and her sister long ago that you can't know for absolutely sure if Alzheimer's is the culprit until an autopsy. And from what Jude read, that part about Alzheimer's hadn't changed. What good would a certain diagnosis do you then, thought Jude, imagining someone cutting into her dead brain and finding an olive pit sitting in a bowl of cobwebs.

But something felt wrong, so Jude told her doctor about the blank spaces, the melted ice cream, the sudden rage at her friends at the lake. And Carly listened and didn't once look away to write a note, but held Jude's hand. And Jude kept going.

"Sometimes at work I suddenly start to panic when I meet a new client that maybe I already know her and I've forgotten."

"Has that really ever happened?"

"No, but I worry that it could."

"Do you feel this way every day, Jude?"

"No, some days I feel perfectly clear and normal. Well, relatively."

"There are many things that can cause forgetfulness and confusion," said Carly. "And there are tests we can do. And some medications we could think about." Carly didn't sound all that alarmed, thought Jude, starting to relax.

"I wish I could take a vitamin or eat some leafy green vegetable and be my old quick self. Got anything like that, Carly?"

"Wish I did, Jude. I could make a fortune."

"What about gingko? Isn't that supposed to be good for the brain," asked Jude.

Carly shook her head. "I think that one's been pretty much disproved. Some say sardines, turmeric, other brain food."

"And don't forget my favorite, red wine," said Jude.

"Oh, yes," said Carly. "We must do our part to keep our local industry healthy." She smiled and asked, "How much red wine are you drinking these days?"

Jude tried to remember the right answer; the one Carly would approve of. "Oh, one glass, sometimes two on special occasions." After all, Carly hadn't asked how much white wine Jude drank.

"Moderation," said Carly, then added, "Some forgetfulness is not unusual, especially as we get older. What are you now, Jude?" She looked at her chart. "68. There's a lot jammed into a 68-year-old brain. And you're probably a multi-tasker like me. We forget to focus. Last week I left the bathroom heater on when I went to work. When I came home for lunch it was like a sauna."

That made Jude felt better, but could she say more? She lowered her voice, like she was telling a secret. "But sometimes I get so scared. I feel like I have lapses. There are pieces that I feel are cut out of my brain and gone, like a jigsaw puzzle piece that got lost under the couch"

"Hmm," said the doctor. "There is something called 'pseudo dementia.'"

"What's that?"

"What happens is that some people, often as we get older... not that you're that old, Jude."

"It's okay, Carly. I'm old. We just agreed I'm 68."

"Okay, anyhow sometimes people develop such severe depression they simply cannot think well. Stress can do that too. We can do something for depression and stress. Jude, you've always been so upbeat and I don't see any big difference in you now, but that doesn't mean you're not depressed."

Jude thought to herself, "You don't know the half of it," as Carly went on.

"I see your weight's up a bit. Are you still getting exercise? Don't you do yoga?"

"Yes, when I feel like it. But a lot of times I don't. Feel like it."

"Okay," said Carly, acting like she was going to wrap up the inquisition.

"One more thing," said Jude. "Did I ever tell you my mother had Alzheimer's? I must have. She had it and we had a great aunt who was truly nutty although no one ever said why. I think about this a lot lately, about how I can't bear to go through what my mother did."

Carly nodded and said softly, "There are some verbal tests we can try. We can do an MRI or CT scan although we cannot identify Alzheimer's with certainty. We can look into eliminating other causes. Make another appointment and we'll get started," said Carly, standing up and hugging Jude, her stethoscope pressing into Jude's breasts. "In the meantime, Jude, do quit scaring yourself." And she added, "You might want to cool it on the wine."

Leaving the clinic, Jude recalled being with her mother when a doctor asked her to name the president of the United States. "Old shit for brains," said her mother, not missing a beat. A lifelong Republican, she at least had remembered she didn't like the current president—a Democrat—even if she couldn't bring up his name. Or maybe she really did know his name and was just trying to get a rise out of her liberal daughter.

Her mother had always been a bit of a kidder. Do you get to keep your sense of humor even when you lose your mind? Jude wondered and realized she was actually in a better mood than when she walked into her doctor's office. She'd been nervous about the appointment but it had gone pretty well. She hadn't told Carly everything but at least she'd said the word Alzheimer's out loud to someone who might not let her take it back, although Carly didn't seem worried enough to get her tested right away. Good, she could wait a little longer.

To celebrate Jude decided to drive to the beach. It was a blue-sky November afternoon, crispy cool and sunny. She'd take the back roads and catch some red and gold vineyards. Fall was Jude's favorite time of year even minus the sharp tang of a Michigan November. She'd go to the beach and take a walk, the best way to clear a fuzzy head.

In the clinic's parking lot, she picked around in her bag for the keys and walked toward her car. Oops, this red car had a child's seat in it. Not hers. She'd parked, where? Could she have been so worried about talking to Carly that she'd completely forgotten? No, all she had to do was breathe and retrace her steps. It couldn't be in the back lot because she never parked there. Where was the damn car? How could she go to the beach if she couldn't find her damn car?

"Excuse me. Ms. Eiler?" said a voice behind her in the parking lot.

Jude jumped and turned around. It was the receptionist, looking at Jude with big helpful eyes. "Is something wrong?"

The receptionist looked so eager and solicitous. She was younger than Jude's own Katy and she was treating Jude like she was some poor, lost old woman. Had the staff been watching Jude from the window as she paced back and forth? Had she been muttering to herself?

"Are you looking for your husband. He..."

Jude cut her off and said evenly. "No, dear. I'm looking for my car and now I remember that I parked it up the street and walked over here."

"What kind of a car do you have, Ms. Eiler?" the young woman asked.

"It's... um. You know. It's red. Compact." What did this kid want from her? What did she mean, what kind of a car?

But then, there it was and someone was driving it and waving at her.

"Hey baby, I've been waiting for you to call me," said her husband, leaning over to open the passenger door.

Jude stared at him—Charlie?—and then back at the receptionist, who gave Jude a cockeyed grin and winked—did she really wink?—at Charlie. Jude quickly read the name on the dashboard. Honda. She sounded out the letters in her head. Yes, yes, of course, Honda.

What was Charlie doing in her car and what was he babbling about?

"You said you'd call when you were finished and after a while I decided to check and see what was going on. I thought maybe your doctor was out on an emergency and you were still waiting. They said you'd already left. Are you okay?"

Why did Charlie have to call her doctor's office? No wonder they'd sent someone out looking for her. Jude didn't want their concern. Or to have them in there whispering about her.

"How come you have the car?" she said, accusingly.

"You remember. My car's in the shop, so I needed yours to run to the store. I dropped you at the doctor's and you were going to call me to come get you."

Now he was looking at her oddly. "Is something wrong? I thought this was just one of those female checkups. Is there something else?"

"No. I'm fine. Silly of me to not remember you had the car. I guess I was thinking about work or something. And yeah, they were running late and then I got into a conversation with that pretty young woman who just winked at you."

She pushed a smile on her face and looked in her bag for her sunglasses. "So, shall we go to the beach?"

"Beach? No way we can do that today," said Charlie. "Katy's coming up for dinner. And you told her you'd make her favorite petrale sole. And a Caesar. I got what you had on the list." He gestured to the grocery bags in the back seat.

CHAPTER EIGHT

FRANNY HAD CALLED JUDE to say they should get together and catch up and Jude had agreed. "But no restaurant. It's getting chilly, but let's meet at Doran."

"Great. Then I can bring Oliver," said Franny. He needs a beach run."

"Shall we ask Anna, too?" asked Jude.

"I don't think so. She's helping Heather settle in."

"Heather?"

"Rick's mother. Changed her name from Helen. Remember? She moved in."

"In with Anna and Rick? In their house?"

"God, yes. Anna's worst nightmare. She didn't tell you?"

"Oh, probably. But I haven't talked to her in a while," said Jude, grabbing a piece of paper and writing down, "Call Anna."

Doran Beach, a long spit of white sand and lush marsh protected from the open ocean, was one of their favorite winter walks. Franny waved her park pass at the ranger as Oliver stuck his yellow head out the car window and eagerly sniffed the salt air.

Franny found Jude stretched out on a sand dune, eyes closed, a green cap pulled low on her forehead, in a thick sweater, down vest and jeans, brown hiking boots tossed to one side. That woman would go barefoot even if she were ice fishing, thought Franny. It was one of Jude's charms, a childlike compulsion to yank off her shoes whenever she got near water. She looked asleep but her mouth twitched slightly.

Franny dropped Oliver's leash, threw a ball and yelled, "Don't get me in any trouble." She lay down next to Jude, seeking warmth from the thin winter sun and the closeness of her old friend. Looking over, she saw a tear on Jude's cheek. "What's going on, sweetie?"

"Sometimes I think I'm beginning to disappear, Franny," said Jude. "Things are happening and my brain feels all wrong. What if my mind is going?"

"Oh Jude, no. Don't say that. This is that same stuff you were talking about on the camping trip. Isn't it? I thought you were just being a little hysterical, after we saw that poor child almost drown, and then, we were all drinking so much."

In fact, that is what Jude blamed her behavior on when she talked to Franny after they got home from the lake. "Sorry to be such an overwrought drama queen," she had said and Franny felt relieved, wanting to believe that was all it was, but now Jude was saying it again.

"I worry all the time. I try not to and then something will happen and I get scared that I'm really sick."

Jude didn't look sick to Franny, and Franny couldn't stand it if she was. Franny counted on Jude to go on forever. Jude liked to refer to herself as, "one tough broad," adding, "I can say that. No one else gets to." Even when Jude had the flu, she acted like it was no big deal. And if Franny or anyone else was sick, Jude would come by with ginger tea and the latest *Vanity Fair*. But there was a limit to Jude's sympathy. After a few days she would say, "Wipe your nose and get on with it. Sick people make me crabby."

Franny reached over and touched Jude's pink face, like a mother searching for a fever. Jude flicked away her tears and stared into Franny's eyes. Franny smiled and Jude smiled back. Then, Franny frowned. And Jude frowned back.

Neither said anything for a while. Looking up, they watched a seagull fight erupt. The two birds yelled at each other as they clamped onto the same piece of old sandwich. Franny wished the noisy birds could direct their displeasure at Jude and screech, "Now, that's enough of that sick talk."

"Franny, you have to help me."

"Of course, I will help. But how? Have you talked to your doctor?"

Jude nodded. "We've talked. She's ruled out a few things. Says I can take some tests."

"So, take the damn tests."

"Well, maybe."

"What about stress?" said Franny, propping up on one elbow. "What you need to do is to quit that crazy making job. Retire. You're almost 70. Stop trying to fix other people's lives."

"Franny, if it's what my mother had I can't live with it."

Jude looked like she was going to cry again and Franny lay back down and put her arms around her. "Jude…please…don't," she whispered. "It's not that. It can't be. I don't know what. But, no. No."

"Will you just keep being my friend?"

Franny hugged her tighter and then Jude switched moods, pulled away, sat up and straightened her clothes. She patted Franny's leg and smiled. "Okay, that's enough. Some tourist is going to come through the dunes and think they've caught two lesbians making out."

Instead, over a megaphone came a voice from a ranger car stopped behind them on the beach road. "Will the owner of the yellow Lab leash him right now?"

"Oh shit. I forgot all about Oliver," said Franny, jumping up and whistling for her dog who was barking at the waves.

"Busted," said Jude, running toward Oliver. She rolled up her jeans and waded into the water.

"Jude, that's got to be freezing."

"It is," said Jude. "It feels fantastic. Makes you know you're alive." She stared out at the ocean and said, "If I'm sick, I'm not going to let myself get much sicker. I'd rather end things my own way. But I might need you, might want you, and maybe Anna to be with me."

"End things?" said Franny, looking around. "What are you talking about? You're going too fast for me. There has to be something else. Not…that."

Jude kept looking at the ocean. "Well, not this minute. That dog sheriff is probably still watching."

"God Jude, you're making me crazy. You're not seriously saying you would do that. Take your own life?"

"Yes, I would. I could. I think about it."

Franny shivered and wrapped her wool scarf tight around her neck. She shook her head and said, "Jude, come on. I know you're afraid but everyone has days when we think we're losing it. It's another crappy part of getting older. I was at a school reception the other day and couldn't remember a woman's name who's been teaching there as long as I have." Franny struggled for other examples of her own faulty memory but Jude held up her hand.

"Franny, I'm worried this is beyond forgetfulness. I'm not always in control. I get lost. I couldn't remember how to figure a 20 percent tip and had to lie that I couldn't read the numbers. And you know how I brag about my math. I'm so afraid of being found out at work. Every time there's some new computer upgrade, I want to throw up."

"Oh, I hate that too."

"Stop, Franny. Just listen. Some days I sit home on the couch, afraid to go anyplace. I've been avoiding you guys. I do things that aren't me. A week ago, I was in Safeway and recognized the husband of one of my clients and I just went off on him, in the produce section. I hate men like him. Why do they think they can hit a woman? Break her bones. Humiliate her. Make her afraid to live. The creep's still walking around. And you know what, Franny? Everyone who heard us looked at me like I should be locked up and not him. If my boss ever found out, I would be fired. Besides, that's not how I do things."

"Well, I don't know that I blame you for losing it, after some of the stories you've told me. But Jude, what about Charlie and Katy?"

"I don't want them to know any of what I've told you. I can't ask either of them to help me because they wouldn't let me do anything to hurt myself. Franny, this will be the hardest part for you, to not let them know. You must swear to me that you won't tell anyone. I have to be able to talk about this and it has to be you. And Anna. I want to tell Anna, too. No one else. You have to trust me. But I can't wait a long time to figure out what to do because I don't know how much longer I can trust myself."

Franny remembered a kid she knew in junior high. She kind of had a crush on him, then his parents sent him away to military school. Franny heard he was having trouble there. He came home that first Thanksgiving and sealed up the garage, got into his father's car and turned the motor on while his parents were away. Franny's mother wouldn't let her go to his funeral. No one ever said why he did it.

Jude bent over and rubbed her face into Oliver's wet fur. "You little scofflaw. Charlie and I were going to get a dog after Dolly died. It's too bad we never did." She kicked at the water. "Charlie lost it when we had to put Dolly to sleep. It surprised me because we both knew that dog wasn't going to get any better. But Charlie was so sad. After the vet gave Dolly the injection, Charlie held her and said, 'It's okay baby, it's okay.' We wrapped Dolly up and took her home and Charlie went out to the sunflower garden with a shovel and dug her a grave, crying the whole time. But lucky Dolly. It was over so quickly and done so gently. How come people don't get to have those kinds of endings?"

Franny started to cry. "I don't want to lose you Jude."

It was Jude's turn to wrap her arms around Franny. "I don't want to lose me either."

CHAPTER NINE

ANNA CHEWED ON A piece of her hair and stared at the cold dry garden from her desk in the kitchen, a breakfast nook she'd turned into an office. It helped to have a pleasant view when you're doing bills and boring paperwork but today there was limited beauty to enjoy. A couple wrinkled strawberries peeked from last year's patch and the hydrangea bushes stood pruned and squat, looking optimistic, Anna thought, even though there wasn't a rain cloud in sight. People were already talking about water rationing.

"Well, I guess we might as well make the most of another beautiful day," said Heather, pouring a cup of coffee. Actually, she chirped it. That was what, Heather, her mother-in-law, born Helen, did. She chirped. It was not going great, this living together.

"I want the sky to turn black and I want it to pour and the windows to rattle," said Anna. "I want the gutters to gush and the streets to flood."

"Well, Anna, you don't have to get so dramatic," said her mother-in-law.

It wasn't just for the sake of the parched earth that Anna wanted the heavens to howl. Anna's dearest friend had told her she wished to die. Just like that, without warning. Well, not entirely. Franny had indicated something was up with Jude, in her short email. "Did you and Jude talk yet?"

Anna immediately called Franny. "What? What's happening now?"

Franny sighed. "Jude and I went to the beach, out to Doran, and had a long talk. A long strange talk, Anna."

"What about?"

"More of that gruesome stuff she was so worried about in the summer. About her mother and death. But she made me promise not to say anything until she talked to you. After she does, call me and we'll get a drink. Several."

Jude had called Anna and asked her to come over. "It's been too long. Let's have tea." The two sat on Jude's rose and gray striped vintage couch with the lumpy cushions that Anna knew well. They sipped Darjeeling from the thin flowered cups they'd found on one of their garage sale forays. A group of passing school kids shrieked to each other and a fire engine wailed from Sebastopol's Main Street as Anna listened to her friend talk about dying.

"Anna, I'm so afraid of what could be happening to me. I think about it all the time and I'd rather die than live with what my mother had."

Anna put her hands around her tea cup and breathed in the warmth. "Jude, I know this has been haunting you but I haven't seen you say or do anything like your mother." She paused, wanting to sound calm and reassuring. "And even if it were Alzheimer's. And really, I don't think it is. I mean, you have us and you have Charlie and Katy and all the other people who love you to help you."

"That sounds nice, Anna, but I would not be the same person and people wouldn't know what to do with me. I'd be like that philodendron over there, sitting in the corner and people would feed me and make sure I had water, maybe even talk to me a little but then walk on by."

"Jude. Oh, Jude. Please don't talk like that."

"Anna, all I want you to know is that I cannot stand to live if I have Alzheimer's. I will have to do something. And you and Franny need to let me."

Jude and Anna had met when they were sampling different exercise programs, including a mutually rejected adult ballet class. "Good lord, what was I thinking. Me in a leotard?" Jude said to Anna as they rushed to their cars after the class ended.

"I'm thinking maybe yoga would be more my style," said Anna and two weeks later she and Jude showed up at the same yoga class at the Y. Jude suggested they go for coffee after and from then on kept up their weekly yoga and coffee, finding a lot in common. Raising kids, protesting oil drilling on the coast, second-hand shopping. They traded titles of books and movies whenever they saw each other and Jude invited Anna into a book club being organized by her friend Franny.

The three had become tight friends along with Martha from the same book club. Meanwhile Jude's and Anna's kids grew into adults. Franny got a divorce. Anna got cancer. Martha died. And Jude, pretty much, saved Anna's marriage.

Back then, Anna was the one falling apart, not because of cancer but because she suspected Rick was seeing someone from work. She showed up one night at Jude's door stoned and crying. Jude listened to Anna's rambling accusations and put together a bed for her on the couch. Jude called Rick and said Anna was too tipsy to drive home which didn't seem to worry him. The next morning Anna told Jude she was going to confront Rick but two weeks later she hadn't. Jude knew Rick only casually, from a few parties, but after Anna had spent several nights on Jude's couch, Jude couldn't stand it anymore. She finally called Rick at work.

"I don't know what you're doing, Rick, but if you are fooling around and Anna asks you to tell her the truth, don't lie. Don't let her think she's going crazy. She's had enough pain and if you try to hide it, she will never forgive you. And I won't either."

Rick protested. "I'm sorry Jude, but I don't want to talk to you about some dumb gossip. I don't want to be rude, but it's really none of your business."

"Wait a minute, Rick," Jude had said, trying to keep her voice even. "If you are doing anything to hurt my friend it is definitely my business. And whether you noticed or not, Anna is hurting."

Rick finally agreed. "Okay, okay, I'll talk to Anna," he said, which led to a long siege that Anna and Rick weathered, thanks to an expensive therapist in San Francisco and Jude.

Months later Rick had come up to Jude at a dinner party, given her an awkward hug, said, "Thank you," and added, "God, you women really hang together."

Now, sitting in Jude's living room, hearing the fear in Jude's voice, seeing the anguish in her face, Anna didn't want to believe what her friend was suggesting. "Jude, are you saying that you are thinking of killing yourself? Committing suicide? I can't let you do that."

Jude looked down and folded her napkin, smoothing the edges. "I always thought maybe I'd die in an accident someday, like Martha. Not that Martha was lucky. Hers was a terrible tragedy, but it was quickly over. For me, dying could be long and wretched, like it was for my mother. I need to make sure that doesn't happen. You faced it, Anna. That you might die. And you didn't die. And your doctors fixed you. But no one can fix me if I have this. It will just get worse."

"What is your doctor telling you, Jude?"

"She says I can wait. She doesn't seem all that worried. She says there could be better tests in the future. That there's a lot of research going on. But I think, what would a test do? There's no cure. I know this probably doesn't make sense but, in a way, I don't want to know." She raked her fingers through her hair. "But sometimes I do want to know. Because then I would do something about it."

"I don't like what you're saying, Jude," said Anna, making herself stop before she told Jude what she believed, that suicide was morally wrong.

Quickly Jude backed off, widened her eyes and smiled. "There are other ways to go, you know, Anna. I could get hit by lightning. Zap, you're gone. The end, thank you Mother Nature."

"How would that possibly be a good way to go?" asked Anna, trying to keep calm when she really wanted to run out of the room and scream.

"I read about these two women swimmers. Somewhere back in the Midwest. Lake Michigan. Terrific thunder and lightning storms. We went to the beach a lot at Lake Michigan when I was a kid. It was as big as an ocean, at least to me. Sand dunes, beach grass. You couldn't see the opposite shore. Fabulous surf." She put her hands together and made a motion like she was diving into a big wave.

"Anyhow, these two women in the news were old friends who were swimming together and must have seen the storm clouds and knew enough to get the hell out of the water. The lifeguards were telling everyone to clear the beach."

She closed her eyes like she was picturing the scene. "So, I imagine the women were not all that scared. Probably talking as they packed up their stuff. You know blankets and books, maybe stopping to put on a sweatshirt or cover-up. They probably had cover-ups. Women wear cover-ups back in Michigan. Something that extends past the thighs. The two women were in their 60s. They probably had on those black serviceable swimsuits that older women wear. Not us, really, but other older women."

This was such a Jude thing, thought Anna, to get caught up in the grimmest stories. And under normal circumstances, Anna would have played along. "Oh yes, and those unattractive swim-caps that serious swimmers wear. You see women like that down at the pool. Hardy types. Doing their vigorous side-stroke."

But this time Anna just let Jude go on.

"According to the report," said Jude, "the women had just reached the boardwalk and were heading to the parking lot when... ka-boom. Lightning got them both. One, two. The lifeguards gave them CPR and ambulances got them to the hospital. But they both died. Lightning stops your heart. They probably didn't feel a thing. That would be okay."

Anna sighed. "We don't get that much lightning here, Jude."

"I know. And even if we did what are the chances of getting hit by it? Ha. Isn't there some joke about that?" She went quiet and then said, "You know what was so very nice about those two women? They'd been having a good time together at the beach. And then it was over. And they didn't die alone."

Anna just sat staring and then said, "Your doctor's not going to help you kill yourself if that's what you're thinking. It's still not legal in California."

"Not yet. We're getting there," said Jude.

"So, you would go to Oregon?"

"Nope. Oregon or any place where assisted suicide is legal

won't work for someone like me," said Jude. "I don't want to get into it now but I think this is something I'll have to do myself. But I hope you and Franny will support me. As much as you can."

"How, Jude? When?"

"I'm still figuring that out." Jude stood up, stretched out her arms, exhaled deeply and walked to her liquor cabinet. "We need some brandy to go in this tea."

As soon as Anna got home, she called Franny. She finished telling the death-by-lightning story and said, "It was so weird. She went from scaring the shit out of me to telling me how lucky these poor women were to die at the beach. And, I have to say for a woman who claims to be losing her memory, she sure had all the details down."

"What do you think she wants us to do?" asked Franny.

"I don't know but I have real objections to suicide," said Anna.

"Like what? Weren't you with me when that guy with the Death with Dignity petition was at the mall?"

"Well yes, I was but I didn't sign it."

"You didn't, Anna?" asked Franny. "I guess we didn't talk about it but I assumed we were, you know, on the same page." She tried kidding her. "What happened? Did you start going to church again or something? Do you think people who die by suicide will burn in hell?"

Anna felt her face get warm. "I don't have to think just like you do, Franny. I was raised Catholic and I'm just not sure."

"I know Anna, but isn't it like abortion? A choice thing? I know how you feel about that. You're not exactly in line with the Pope."

Anna blew her nose. "I don't know what I feel, what I think. But Franny, we're not just talking about anyone's decision to end their life. We're talking about Jude."

"Well, I think it has to be a personal decision," said Franny, sounding more reasonable than she felt. This was not a friendly safe debate over the pros and cons of suicide like she might have with her students. This was becoming frighteningly personal.

They were both silent and then Anna said, "We'll get those

drinks. What night are you free?"

"Any time next week," said Franny. "This weekend I'm supposed to go to some dumb birthday party."

Chapter Ten

Franny didn't like going to parties by herself, especially when she wasn't sure who else was going to be there but she felt kind of pressured into this one. The invitation had come from Julia, whose husband Steve used to work with Franny's ex-husband. They'd done couple things together and after Franny and Tim divorced the two women stayed in touch. They had recently run into each other at the movies when Julia told Franny she was having a surprise 60th birthday party for Steve. She'd followed with an email, "See you Saturday." Franny wrote back, "Looking forward," already thinking of excuses not to show up.

She could always say she'd been up all night with some stomach bug. Or use one of her favorite lies about an old college roommate suddenly being in town.

By the time you reached middle age a person had a good list of dependable excuses. And with email you could just dash off an apology rather than having to fib on the phone, especially to a second-tier friend like Julia.

With a close friend you could tell the truth. If it were Jude or Anna, Franny could call and say, "I'm just not in the mood. I don't like feel like a party. I'd be lousy company." They'd understand.

But all this talk about dying had made Franny feel very lonesome. Another night with Oliver and Masterpiece wasn't going to help. She'd go to the stupid party, drink a little, flirt a little and forget about death and disease.

She put on her favorite black dress, a couple of turquoise and silver necklaces from her mother's Santa Fe collection and pulled on black tights and her tallest black boots. At the last minute she exchanged the black tights for pale blue. Maybe some attractive stranger at the party would think she looked the arty type. If she did meet anyone exciting tonight, she'd say she was a writer. It was kind of true.

Franny made it a point to never get to a party until an hour after it started. Her mother, an expert in social strategy, said, "People look too eager when they show up on time, like it's the only date on their calendar."

The living room, decorated with the predictable black balloons, was filling with middle-aged revelers when Franny walked in. Julia gave her a quick air kiss and pointed to the bedroom where she could drop her coat and bag. Franny was always curious about people's sleeping arrangements, wondering who slept on which side and whose table had the better pile of books. The new Elizabeth George. Must be Julia's side. And what a humongous bed. Did everyone today own beds that were wider than they were long? Franny and Oliver were quite cozy in her standard double.

Franny looked in the mirror, fluffed her short curls and touched up the dark red lipstick which emphasized her still full lips. One of the perks of not smoking cigarettes when you were young, she thought. Fewer mouth lines. She smiled, following more motherly advice to look in the mirror and say "Beautiful." Franny didn't have her mother's confidence but she held the smile and walked out of the bedroom and heard giggles.

Tim stood in the hallway with a woman. "Well, look who's here," he said, giving her that half smirk she'd lived with for 12 years. "Franny, meet Gillian," said Tim, dropping an arm around a dark-haired woman in glasses, the kind of designer frames Franny's health plan would never cover.

"Gillian, meet Franny, my ex-wife."

Gillian, presumably the giggler, looked 15 years younger than Tim, and therefore Franny.

The women shook hands. Franny felt a big ring on Gillian's right hand but saw nothing on the left hand. She pointed her chin up toward Tim to accept a kiss on the cheek. They chatted briefly and Franny broke away to find a glass of wine.

Of course, her ex would be at the party, because he and Steve might still work together. But it was always a bit unsettling to see Tim. It didn't happen often, there being no practical need to stay in touch. Tim did look pretty good, though, in a corduroy jacket-blue jeans sort of way.

He had started dating almost immediately after they split up, which had offended Franny who thought that even though theirs was a so-called amicable divorce it would seem to be only good manners to observe a mourning period before racing into the playing field.

It was Jude's opinion that men cannot stand to be alone. "Especially the boys of our generation. They marry young and pretty soon start to act like they're trapped and as soon as the trap is sprung, they're back out there, looking for another woman to nest with. And pretty soon, complaining about being in another trap."

Tim had remarried within a year of their divorce. He invited Franny to the wedding which she thought was pushing it, even for California. The marriage didn't last and now here was the latest girlfriend. Franny wished she had brought a date but there were no current candidates.

Julia came walking towards her, looking eager. "You see Tim?"

"Yep. We kissed. On the cheek. He introduced me to Gillian. Nice glasses," she said, withholding further commentary." If Julia was hoping for some gossipy discomfort between the ex-spouses, Franny wasn't going to deliver. It had been too long a time, anyhow, for leftover drama. Certainly, neither she nor Tim pined for the other after all those years.

Julia suddenly shh-ed everyone and announced that Steve was on his way and everyone had to hide in the back rooms. Franny quickly poured another glass of wine and started to back up towards the hallway when someone yanked on her arm and pulled her into a closet.

He smelled of mint. Had he popped an Altoid or had he taken to wearing some new scent favored by single men in their late 50s pursuing 40-year-olds?

"I was hoping you'd be here tonight," he said into her ear.

"Where's your girlfriend?" asked Franny.

"In the bathroom," he said. "It's just you and me."

When everyone yelled surprise, Franny didn't budge. She leaned against Tim, just to see what he would do. One hand came around and cupped her breast. She stood there, more than a little bit excited.

"Talk about surprises," she whispered and slowly turned to kiss him on the lips. And he kissed back. Tim had been particularly good at long, deep kisses.

But now what were they supposed to do? The crowd noises moved into another room and Franny slowly opened the closet door, guiltily looking around. Tim whispered, "Well, that was nice," as he squeezed by Franny and headed toward the guest of honor.

A few days later Anna met Franny who sat waiting at a table in the bar at a Mexican restaurant. They hugged and Anna fingered Franny's crimson scarf. "I don't know this scarf. It looks good on you. In fact, you look great."

"Thanks, darling. I already ordered for us."

The waiter delivered a pitcher of happy hour margaritas, said "Enjoy" and poured two glasses. Franny leaned across the table toward Anna and said, "I know we're here to talk about Jude but first I have to tell you what happened at the party." Anna grinned as Franny recounted her moment in the closet with her ex. Anna knew Franny had had several boyfriends since her divorce, but lately Franny had admitted to being lonesome and "horny, definitely horny."

"You and old Tim, who would think?" said Anna. "Although I always thought of him as pretty good looking. Kind of sexy. But I thought you were relieved to be rid of him."

"I was. I am. Who knows? Right now, I'm starving," said Franny her mouth full of tortilla chip. She grabbed for the salt shaker. "Yuk. These things are awful."

"I think they're supposed to be healthy. No gluten. No salt. No taste," said Anna, piling a fat scoop of salsa on a chip. "This helps. Tell me more."

"I think it surprised us both, but there we were kissing and rubbing up against each other. In the dark. Smashed against the coats."

"Well, well. You know, I read somewhere that different milestone events turn people on. Weddings. Birthdays. You said it was Tim's friend's 60th birthday. Maybe Tim was feeling time slipping away."

"Tim's definitely breathing hard on 60," said Franny. "He was there with his young girlfriend."

"You know what else I read makes people horny? Death."

"Really? You are a fountain of fascinating information, Anna."

"Think about it. Someone dies and you decide you better grab it all while you can and maybe that includes the first warm body."

"Like, screw you, death."

"Exactly. I think even a close call with dying is a turn-on. I know after my first breast cancer scare Rick and I couldn't get enough of each other."

She turned quiet and loaded up another chip. "For a while, at least."

Franny knew the rest of that story. Then had come Anna's next cancer and then Rick's affair and then the near split-up.

"But you two are okay now?"

"Yeah, I guess," said Anna." Except now we have Mommy Dearest living with us."

A young woman waved from the bar; a student Franny recognized from school. Franny gave her a weak smile, not welcoming enough to draw her to their table. She wanted Anna to herself.

Pulling her notebook from her bag, Franny said, "This is good stuff. I've got to remember to look all this up. Death, birthdays, weddings, funerals and sex. Sounds like a Woody Allen movie."

"Yep. But it's not like we haven't had our fill of death talk lately," said Anna. "Thanks to our dear Jude. I swear I wake up thinking about her every morning."

"Me, too," said Franny, although truthfully, she hadn't thought of Jude at all that morning because there was an eager warm body next to her that wasn't Oliver the dog. Good old Tim. She would love to tell Anna about that development but Anna had switched to Jude.

"I don't know. She seems to be so convinced that she's getting like her mother," said Anna. "But I'm not sure I believe it."

"You don't believe Jude has Alzheimer's?" asked Franny. "Or

you don't believe Jude believes she has Alzheimer's?"

"I believe she is very worried and I believe she is scaring herself to death," said Anna. "I know she's scaring me. But I wonder how much of this is in Jude's head?"

Franny grimaced. "Well that's the problem isn't it? Jude's pretty sure that what's in her head is Alzheimer's."

"Franny, you know what I mean. Is it possible that Jude could be imagining it all?"

"I don't know," said Franny. "Something's making her feel pretty crazy. She gets so sad and then almost panicky and starts thinking Alzheimer's." She patted her notebook. "I've started to do some research on it. You know it's called the Baby Boomers nightmare?"

"I do get that," said Anna. "We're all afraid of our memories going. Rick said something the other day about CRS."

"Huh?"

"CRS—can't remember shit," said Anna. "Kind of funny, I guess. Write that down, too. I even asked Rick's mother about Alzheimer's. The other night at dinner. Just asked if she knew anyone who had it. She acted horrified. Looked at me as if I asked if any of her friends had the clap."

"How old is Heather? In her late-80s, easily. Right?"

Anna nodded. "Good lord, don't say that to her, but yes, she's up there."

"Well then, by now she's got to have known at least a few people with Alzheimer's," said Franny.

"That's what I assumed," said Anna, "but she shut me right down and Rick changed the subject."

The waiter drained the pitcher into their empty glasses. "Anything more, ladies?"

Franny looked up at him and shook her head. "I don't think so. And thanks for not calling us girls."

"Ladies is better than girls?" asked Anna. "Since when?"

The waiter smiled and Franny fished a slice of lime from the bottom of her glass. "Okay, Anna, you and I need to figure out how to help Jude."

"I wish we could talk to Charlie. Or Katy, at least," said Anna. "You and Katy are close and you said she already told you she was worried about her mother."

"I know, but Jude made us promise to not tell anyone."

"That's asking a lot of us," said Anna. "I'd do anything to help Jude. But I'm not going to help her kill herself and that's what it sounds like she's asking us. I can't do that. It's wrong."

"Like, immoral?"

"Yes, a crime against God. Yes, that's what I do think, Franny."

"Oh Anna, there you go again, getting all religious on me."

Anna shook her head and took a last sip of margarita to calm herself. "Franny, that's not really fair. You and I have to be able to talk about this without you questioning or mocking my beliefs."

Franny looked away and Anna continued. "All my life the church has said suicide is wrong and now my friend is possibly asking me to help her die. Or let her kill herself?"

She picked up her empty glass, frowned and set it down hard on the table.

"What about you, Franny? Is it okay with you? You going to help Jude kill herself?"

"Fuck, I don't know," said Franny, slumping back in her chair. "I'm sorry. I guess we have to figure out what Jude wants from us. Let her talk about it so she doesn't feel alone. I don't think she would ask us to do something illegal."

"I don't know what to think," said Anna.

The after-work crowd was getting noisy and likely having a lot more fun conversation than theirs, thought Anna, sliding her chair closer to Franny. "There was something Jude said to me about Oregon. I actually mentioned it to her—kind of lightly. Something like, so Jude, are you going to move to Oregon? And Jude said that wouldn't work for her. She said that Oregon or any place that allows death with dignity, assisted suicide... whatever you call it can't help her. Do you know what she means?"

"I think so. I looked it up, what you have to do in Oregon, and I imagine it will be the same in California if we ever get it. You have to show you have your wits about you so that doctors will know you mean it when you say you want them to help you die. You need to be of sound mind when you do it."

"Oh jeez," said Anna, "and if you have Alzheimer's you're not of sound mind. Is that it? This is too damned awful."

Franny nodded yes. Then she snorted a laugh, tapped a finger on her teeth and pointed to Anna's mouth "Salsa."

Anna swiped her tongue across her teeth and smiled big. "Did I get it?"

"Nope, still there."

Anna wiggled her tongue some more.

"Okay?"

"No," Franny snorted again. "Moved to the front."

Anna covered her mouth and headed, laughing, for the restroom.

Good, thought Franny. We're laughing. That made her think of Jude, who insisted that friends are obligated to watch out for food stuck in teeth, gray hair on black sweaters and wayward chin hairs.

Anna was still smiling when she sat back down and a voice said, "Well, hello girls. Funny running into you here. And it's Anna. You're as lovely as always."

"You too, Tim," said Anna, watching him bend to kiss Franny on the cheek and let his hand rest on her neck.

Chapter Eleven

For years Jude woke up thinking of her mother Ruthie back in Michigan in that building with the white pillars, silent grounds and loud clanging hallways. The care was adequate. Jude's sister Patsy, a nurse, lived nearby and knew some of the staff. "No one's going to mess with Mom," she assured Jude.

Their mother lived there long enough to become a favorite, even once voted Miss Congeniality of Country Pines. "I didn't ask who voted for her, if it was the staff or the other inmates," Jude's sister had said when she called with the latest news about their mother.

"I hope she told them she'd prefer being addressed as Ms. Congeniality," said Jude, fighting a sick feeling in her stomach.

The home gave Ruthie a plastic heart on a pink ribbon. Jude imagined her mother sitting there looking puzzled while some perky nurse put it around her neck. It was so terribly sad.

"I don't know. That's actually sweet," said Charlie when he found Jude crying after talking to her sister. "That's a nice thing for your mother."

"No, it's not," Jude had barked. "It's pathetic." If she could have, Jude would have flown right then to Country Pines and ripped the damned thing off her mother's neck.

Jude worried about her mother not getting her morning coffee. Her mother liked her coffee hot and black in a "real coffee cup with a saucer," preferably the pale green cups that matched her best china. She never took to coffee mugs because she said the coffee cooled off too fast. She liked strong coffee in small cups that she drank in ladylike sips. In the nursing home Jude suspected that coffee came late, weak and tepid in a Styrofoam cup. Or never at all.

Jude hated that her mother had to live in a nursing home. Even after her mother died it took Jude a long time to remember her any other way than sitting in a wheelchair, hair flat to her head, eyes blank, not speaking, as captive as a POW.

Jude tried to replace that last image in favor of happier memories before her mother got sick, but the sad ones would creep in like Marley's ghost. Jude knew why. It was because Jude felt guilty that she didn't try harder to find a gentler, worthier place for her mother than the dementia unit of Country Pines. It was also because Jude had secretly wished, even prayed every night, for her mother to die long before her body finally gave up.

Shitty shit shit, thought Jude, startled to look up at the kitchen clock. She'd been thinking dark thoughts about her mother and now look; her own coffee had turned cold. How long had she been sitting here? A whole hour? She should be taking a shower, getting her day together. Or outside tending to the new drought-tolerant plants. Or leaving a message for Charlie about dinner plans. Was she supposed to be going into work today? No, she had taken the day off. To do what? The wall calendar said "Anna lunch."

On one visit to Michigan Jude walked into Country Pines and spotted her mother down the long hallway, sitting in a chair in a purple robe, slumped over, head down. As Jude approached, her mother slowly raised her head and looked up at Jude. This was back when her mother could still talk. She lifted her thin arms as Jude knelt down to receive her embrace. Ruthie cupped Jude's face and said, "Now I know who I am."

When they were younger people had long remarked on how much her mother and Jude were alike. Not only because of their curly auburn hair and long nose, but they laughed the same, read the same mysteries, clipped the same newspaper recipes, even traded sun dresses and sandals on a beach vacation they took when Jude graduated from college. People would meet them and say things like, "Well, the acorn didn't fall far from the tree."

Jude, who from the time she was a little girl thought her

mother the most beautiful woman in the world, loved being compared to her. Until her mother got sick. Could she have her mother's throaty laugh and not have her disease? Could she look like her, fear cats like her, prefer her eggs scrambled with hot peppers just like Ruthie, but not end up alone in a room where the TV never shuts off? Could the wonderfulness of Ruthie live in Jude without the Alzheimer's part?

Jude had talked to a minister, Reverend Victoria, who came to Jude's office regularly to counsel some of her clients.

"Can I ask you something, Vickie? I've kind of fallen away from the church but my mother was a loyal believer. She sang in the choir, saved her best flowers from the garden for the altar. She put on rummage sales and church suppers. She made my sister and me go to Sunday school. Now we've lost her."

"I'm sorry. When did your mother die?" Vickie said, laying her hand on Jude's.

"She's not dead," said Jude. "She has Alzheimer's."

The minister, a kind and eager sort, told her it's hard to understand God sometimes but no matter how sick Jude's mother was she was still her mother.

That's the part Vickie didn't get. Ruthie wasn't still her mother. Her mother had mostly disappeared except for a confused ghostly version of herself. Where was the rest of her hiding? Had she been cut in two? Was her once-engaged spirit hovering in the ceiling corner of her Country Pines bedroom, like people describe when they're having an out of body experience? Was the healthy Ruthie looking down on her ruined self and saying, "Hey Ms. Congeniality, can't we just get this over with?"

After one of her visits to Michigan Jude told her sister, "I make sure to walk with purpose after I leave Mom's room. I smile at all the nurses and say thank you and goodbye. I don't want anyone thinking I belong there. Can you imagine if some orderly came up and put his arm around me and said, "Now dear, come with me, it's time to go back to your room" while I'm frantically trying to find my visitor's badge. I always take the stairs when I'm leaving. I don't want to get stuck in the elevator and end up on the locked floor."

Okay, enough, Jude told herself and walked into her bedroom

to change. The bedside radio was still on and a reporter was interviewing a Palestinian. Or was it an Iraqi? Could have been Afghani. She had gotten so far behind in the news. She used to care so much. Now all she worried about was herself.

The man, speaking through a translator, said that there had been a bombing in the next village the night before. He knew that his home, all he had, could blow apart at any time. "I fear tomorrow," said the man.

"I know what you mean," Jude said.

Chapter Twelve

Her mother-in-law was doing the *Times* crossword puzzle when Anna walked into the living room, sorted through the papers for the Arts section and aimed for the deck with a cup of coffee.

"Come sit with me, Anna," said Heather, dressed for the day in a mauve cashmere sweater and multiple gold bangles. "We haven't talked much since I got here. I miss our long chats."

Anna, still in her gardening jeans, thought to herself, "Really? You miss our talks, which ended years ago. How is that two people can do major battle and one stays pissed off and the other acts like it was a minor forgettable tiff."

"Anna, the other night you asked me if I knew anyone who had Alzheimer's. I did. I had a couple of friends whom I'm pretty sure had it but called it something else. One woman's children insisted their mother had a tumor, even though she sure acted and looked like what I think of as Alzheimer's. Her obituary said brain cancer."

"That's ridiculous," said Anna, ready to challenge anything her mother-in-law said.

"I guess they were ashamed to say Alzheimer's. Or terrified. I don't know why cancer would be more acceptable than Alzheimer's. Especially once the person is dead. Funny. Anyhow, I wanted to tell you about another friend, a very lovely man whom I played bridge with back home. One day he folded his cards, stood up and said that's it. And he left my house and never played bridge with us again. He did become a little odd. Decided he wanted to be a hiker, spent a fortune at L.L.Bean.

Then he started playing the ukulele. He let his hair grow long. We thought he might have dementia. It worried his wife to death. Then he announced he was flying to Bruges. He told his wife she could come or not. He had been dreaming about a Belgian waffle. And guess what?"

Anna sighed and put down the newspaper. "What?"

"They went to Bruges. And he was walking across the street, heading for a museum or art gallery, I don't remember. And he was hit by a taxi. And that was it."

"He died?" said Anna.

"Yes. And here's the best part. His wife had an autopsy done on him and his brain showed no evidence of Alzheimer's."

"So, what was it?"

"No one ever figured it out. Maybe he was just bored and looking for adventure. Anyhow, he got his Belgian waffle," she said and started to giggle.

Anna couldn't help herself and smiled.

"Oh, good. I'm so glad you liked my story," said Heather, clapping her hands.

Rick's mother was Helen before she became Heather. She changed her name, she'd said, because it sounded "more interesting, more blonde." It was confusing to Rick because his mother had always asked him to call her Helen rather than Mother or Mom. And then she was Heather. Rick's father, Bill, had always referred to his wife as "Heavenly H" so it didn't bother him when she changed it, although occasionally he would roll his eyes at Rick when his wife introduced herself. Anna had no problem with the name change. She actually thought it suited her mother-in-law's personality, but that was back when she was still charmed by her.

When Bill was dying, he made Rick promise to make sure his mother wasn't lonely. "She's a great old gal but she needs lots of attention and love."

After Bill died Anna and Rick told Heather she was welcome to visit whenever she felt like it. But on one of those long visits, Anna learned that Heather had deceived her.

They had become good pals, indulging in long lunches with

Heather's favorite Manhattans. Anna would tell people she never understood why people made so many nasty mother-in-law jokes. She adored Rick's mother. Really, like a second mother to her, since her own had died.

Rick would tease, "So do you girls get together and talk about me?"

"No Ricky, we talk about our other men," said Heather.

Anna made sure Rick bought his mother something elegant for birthdays and Christmas. "With a label she'll recognize."

Anna and Heather were both a little in love with Jeremy Irons and would rent videos of his old films when Heather visited. "Perfect for you, Anna," said Heather after they fell back into the couch swooning, after re-watching *The French Lieutenant's Woman*. "A little young for me but I'd still take him home in a minute."

Anna talked to her mother-in-law about hot flashes, about her son Robby doing drugs. She called Heather first when she found the lump in her breast. Before she told Rick. Even before her friends. But their mutual adoration ended after Rick had his affair and Heather admitted she knew about it.

It was at one of their lunches. Anna told her mother-in-law she didn't feel like shopping but needed lunch so they could talk. As soon as they sat down Anna blurted out, "Heather, you're going to be shocked by this but Rick has been having an affair. With a woman at work. He said it's over but it started while I was recovering. After my mastectomy."

Her mother-in-law hadn't gasped. She didn't cry. She didn't say "that son of a bitch." She didn't jump up to hug Anna. She gave her a sad smile and took her hand.

"Oh honey. I know."

Anna had felt a chill. "What do you mean, you know? You know now? Or did you know then? When did you know?"

It turned into a short lunch. In fact, it was their last. But before Anna walked out of the restaurant, she quizzed her. "Did Rick tell you? And you decided I didn't need to know?"

"I could tell something was going on and I asked him," said Heather. "He was acting just like his father when Bill had his escapade with the neighbor across the street. That was the year we suddenly picked up and moved. Remember? Men do these things. They're weak. They get scared when they start to get old. It's like what Olympia Dukakis says in *Moonstruck* about why men chase younger women, that it's because they're afraid of dying. Rick was devastated when you got cancer. Absolutely terrified."

"Rick was terrified? Well I was pretty terrified myself, Heather."

"I know. It was so hard for you, but he was so afraid of losing you. And being left."

"That's bullshit, Heather," said Anna, pulling sunglasses out of her bag and getting into her coat. "Did he tell you who she was? Did he ask you to cover for him? Did you meet her? Did he tell you they had great sex while I was walking around with drains coming out of my chest? Why didn't you tell me, Heather?"

"Oh, Anna," said Heather, starting to cry. "I thought it would pass and he would come to his senses, which he has. I'm so sorry, darling."

And that was the end of that friendship. Now Heather was living with Rick and Anna and probably would until she died. But Anna could never trust her again. Heather was Rick's mother, her mother-in-law, but she was not Anna's friend. Anna's real friends were Jude and Franny.

Chapter Thirteen

Franny tried not to think too hard about where this was going with Tim. It would just be a fling. It had been a dry spell, dry enough that Franny had, the day after the party, gone to the health store for a jar of Vital Vulva, anticipating what might happen. Which it did that next week when Tim invited himself over, "Just to catch up, see your new place."

Franny felt shy over the prospect of being naked in front of him, worried he might start comparing the before and after Franny. He'd once known her 30-something body and now was exploring the current version, almost twice that age.

One point in his favor, he didn't object when Franny said, "You know we have to use something."

"Oh, sure, I'm a modern guy," he said, pulling a condom from his jeans pocket. "I know about HIV and other things. I've been given the lecture."

Franny gave him an at-a-boy smile.

Tim told Franny she was beautiful. He admired her smooth hips, even her tummy which no amount of sucking in, "zipping the zipper" as her yoga instructor called it, could flatten. He complimented her spiky hair and her house, even becoming misty-eyed when he recognized different furniture pieces.

"Didn't we have this mirror in our dining room," he said, looking into the glass and smoothing his mustache. "Your grandmother gave it to us for a wedding gift."

"Nope. Your sister."

Tim had more hair on his back and less on his head than before and he winced and rubbed one knee getting in and out of bed. But he had become a more inventive lover over the years, for which Franny felt more gratitude than jealousy toward whoever had inspired his new slow moves that left her gasping and laughing out loud.

"You still like this?" she said, straddling him and letting her breasts drop into his hands. When she arched her back and smiled at the ceiling he said, "Impressive."

"Ustrasana. The camel pose."

"Huh?"

"Yoga," she said.

Franny decided to keep Tim a secret for a while, although his visits were becoming regular. "What about Gillian? Isn't she suspicious?" asked Franny, feeling only a little guilty about distracting Tim from another woman.

"She's not really a full time serious girlfriend," said Tim of the chic woman he'd introduced her to at the party. "It's not like we live together."

Still, Franny liked thinking of herself as having a hot affair. Maybe she'd write about it someday. *Sneaking out with your ex.* Her notebooks were getting full, now including sex, and she found herself smiling at odd moments. Her poet friend Holly looked across her desk one day. "Franny, you're looking mighty frisky this morning."

In any other circumstance Franny would have told Jude first. But what would this new Jude say? She was pretty sure the old Jude, the normal Jude, would whoop and holler and demand all the juicy details. Jude preached that sex was good therapy and a boon for the complexion. She's the one who had discovered Vital Vulva, "the favorite lube for women of a certain age." Yes, Jude would approve of Franny having sex but probably not with Tim. She'd call her on it. She'd say something like, "Tell me you're not really thinking of getting back together? You can do so much better."

"Hey, Ms. Franny Gordon, how are you this fine morning," shouted a white-haired man in a cowboy hat and dark glasses sitting in a wheelchair outside the student center. He lifted his glasses and smiled.

"Hey Jeffrey," said Franny, recognizing a popular math professor, also known, in his words, as "Disability activist and all-around shit disturber."

"What's got your blood pressure up these days?" asked Franny, noting the pile of brochures in his lap.

"Same one we disagreed on years ago. Now they call it death with dignity." He snorted. "Still suicide."

Interesting coincidence, thought Franny, bending down to hug Jeffrey." Well, friend, it looks like it could happen finally in California. They're trying real hard to push it through the legislature. This time they might get it."

"Over my dead legs," he said, patting his thighs.

Franny pulled a chair over and said, "And I still think it's a matter of choice. Tell me again, what's wrong with ending your life if there's nothing left?"

"That's an individual thing. This is about sanctioning assisted suicide with a law, to instituting euthanasia as a social policy. And that would be catastrophic. "

"But some people's conditions are catastrophic."

"Yes, and some people probably look at me and think that my life is a catastrophe." Franny knew Jeffrey's story, how he'd been shot in the back when he was a young kid, by a cousin who found a gun in his grandfather's night table. Jeffrey had been in a wheelchair for probably 50 years. His other favorite cause was fighting the NRA.

"Okay, Franny. Nothing's changed. I still believe the same I did back when Jack Kevorkian, good old Dr. Death, was hooking his patients up to his euthanasia machine. What a crackpot. I called him a serial killer in the press. Remember that? It was a good line."

Franny nodded. "But he did get people thinking about how they might be able to get their doctor to help them when there's no hope."

"No hope? I say there is always hope. I can imagine someone looking at me and thinking I should kill myself. Hitler used to call us disabled folks useless eaters."

"Oh God, Jeffrey. Nobody would think that of you." Franny actually considered Jeffrey a perfect example of pride and independence. A colleague described him as "The disabilities access poster stud." Good looking, smart, funny. Franny wondered how Jeffrey and his girlfriend, an artist who showed her work at the college, made love. What were the mechanics? Would it be as sexy as Jon Voight and Jane Fonda in *Coming Home*?

"This whole choice in dying, I think, plays to our fear, well, most people's fear, that the worst thing that could happen to you is to have to ask someone else to wipe your ass, lift you into bed. I hate the assumption that people would rather be dead than disabled. I have a friend, with CP, who's in a chair. She has a T-shirt that says "Please Do Resuscitate."

"Wow," said Franny, smiling at how deftly Jeffrey made what he must have thought was his final point. But she had more to ask.

"What about people who don't want to be a burden on their family?"

Jeffrey put his hand on her leg and his dark eyes flared. "Do they ask their family if they will be a burden?"

Franny sighed. "I don't have kids, Jeffrey, but I understand not wanting to have them see you helpless. What do you say to that?"

Jeffrey shrugged and held up his hands. "I say, tough. You play the cards you're dealt. Could be there are other adventures to come."

"Okay, Jeffrey, what about the person whose mind is gone? Like, someone with Alzheimer's? What adventure is left for her? Him? That person?"

Jeffrey nodded. "I admit, Alzheimer's is tricky. Maybe you get someone with dementia into a day program. Or one of those places with a memory unit."

Franny couldn't imagine Jude in a day program or anything called a memory unit.

"Could you do it, Franny?" asked Jeffrey. "Ask for the pills. Decide what day you're going to die?"

"Me? I don't know. I talk a good line but I'm pretty much an all-around scaredy-cat."

"Well, think on it. It's something we should all be thinking about. It's going to affect everyone if this thing happens," he said, wheeling over to hail a group walking out of the student union.

CHAPTER FOURTEEN

FRANNY CHIDED HERSELF AS she pulled out of the parking garage and headed to Occidental for her quarterly glycolic peel and facial. Here I am, zipping off to drop $100 to fix my wrinkles after arguing suicide with a man in a wheelchair.

Marianna's Redwood Spa was a small cabin in a clearing in the woods. "It's like something Goldilocks would discover," Franny told people, many of whom became Marianna regulars and who, like Franny, believed that facials were part of basic maintenance. As Franny liked to say, "It's the same as taking care of your car. You patch the dents and keep it clean, hoping no one will notice how old the poor thing really is."

Marianna opened the door in a cloud of lavender and mint and the two women hugged. Franny helped herself to chamomile tea and changed into a pink terry cloth wrap as Marianna fiddled with her iPod. "Waterfalls, birds or Buddha bells?"

"Bells," said Franny.

"Talk now or later?" asked Marianna.

"I guess later," said Franny, sinking into the cushioned table under a skylight that framed feathery clouds and ancient trees.

Unlike Franny's chatty hairdresser, Marianna understood a client's need for occasional quiet. Franny closed her eyes and considered Jeffrey's last question. What would she do if she thought living was too painful? Would she take the pills, choose a day to die? All this time she'd been thinking about dying in terms of Jude's crazy talk. But what would Franny do if she became very ill or terribly disabled? Could she bear to have someone wipe her ass, as Jeffrey so prettily put it? Would she want to pull the plug? After a lecture at the college on advanced directives and living wills Franny had filled out the forms about what to do if she became incapacitated. No, she did not want futile medical treatment and yes, she would prefer to die at home. Of course she would want those things. Who wouldn't? But they had seemed like such far off considerations, and she'd filled out the papers almost automatically, like she would a DMV form. Naturally, she had named Jude and Anna as the ones to speak for her if she couldn't.

Franny listened to the tinkling bells and felt Marianna work in the cool sandy lotion that was supposed to slough off dead cells from her tired skin. But her touch couldn't keep Franny's grim thoughts away. What, she wondered, was going to kill her in the end? Strokes ran in her family. Her mother died days after having hers, sparing her family the difficult decision of what to do to keep her going. What if Franny had a stroke and survived but was partially paralyzed? What if she couldn't talk or walk?

"I'm going to pluck some of these wayward eyebrow hairs. Just the white ones," said Marianna. "But first I'd like to massage your forehead. You're all bunched up."

"I'm just thinking about a lot of stuff," said Franny who usually didn't spend much time on health worries. She had some low back pain. Went through a bout with plantar fasciitis. Carpal tunnel stuff in her wrist. She didn't obsess over a disease killing her but people doing her in were another matter. Franny could make herself sick reading the news—murderers, rapists, kidnappers, wrong way drivers like the one who killed Martha. Franny refused to watch crime shows or read murder mysteries. They all seemed to start the same: A woman's nude dead body found in the trunk of a car.

"Do you ever worry about living out here in the woods?" Franny asked Marianna, deciding she did want to talk.

"You mean bad guys? No. I worry more about one of these magnificent trees coming down in a big storm," said Marianna. "Or fire, or an earthquake. I love nature but she can take a mean turn, you know? I just try to live for the moment."

"There was a kid who broke into a house in my neighborhood," said Franny. "In the middle of the day, this woman, a retired nurse, came out of her shower and there was this boy, a teenager. Standing there. Staring at her. I would have died right then and there, Marianna."

"So, what happened."

"Well, she screamed. See, I couldn't have screamed. I'd have frozen. Anyhow, she did scream. The kid ran. She called the cops. They found the kid. He was a new resident of the group home a couple streets over. Got the wrong house."

"Well, then, it all turned out okay," said Marianna, patting Franny's shoulder.

Franny opened her eyes to see Marianna's perfectly exfoliated face hovering above.

"Hey, I saw your friend Jude not long ago." said Marianna.

"Hmm?" said Franny.

"She seemed a little off. Is she okay?"

"Yes," said Franny, feeling her stomach turn. "Sure. Why?"

"Well, I was massaging her face like I usually do at the end. Tapping her forehead, lightly touching her third eye. And she started crying, not sobbing, just a few tears. I asked her if she was okay and gave her a tissue. She didn't move or brush off her tears or say anything for a while. She just lay there. Then she thanked me, got up and changed into her clothes. Then, when we were settling up the bill, she asked me if I ever worked on dead people."

"Dead people?"

"She said she knew I sometimes do make-up for weddings and she wondered if I do funerals. She said she read about a woman who had her friends practice doing her makeup on her when she was alive so they'd use the right blush on her when she died. Then she said, 'I'd like you to practice doing my face some day, Marianna.' I didn't know what to say. But then she laughed like it was a joke."

"Well, that was probably it, Marianna. A joke. Jude does have a black sense of humor," said Franny, not wanting to get into a Jude discussion.

Dressing to leave, Franny smiled at her newly buffed reflection. If she died right now, she'd make a dewy corpse.

How did Marianna and her husband afford such a gorgeous

site, wondered Franny as she slowly drove down a long dirt road to a main road. Obviously, they bought it long ago before prices went nuts. This would be a perfect site for one of Anna's communes, Franny thought. Anna had visited a community of retired people in Mendocino County, "cool old hippies," and decided she and her friends should start one. That was years ago but Anna continued to promote the idea. She'd spot some property in her real estate listings and say, "Here's five acres not too far from the ocean where we could do our Geezer-ville."

Of course, they would continue on together, in some way. After watching *The Best Exotic Marigold Hotel*, Jude had declared, "That's what we'll do. Move to an exotic country with other eccentrics and have sex with their discarded husbands."

To do any of that meant they would have to stay healthy and fit, so they would often share stories on durable old women they could model themselves after. One of Franny's favorites was a New York City octogenarian runner who came in first in the age 80 to 99 division and told a reporter she had 20 years to go.

"See, we can do this too," Franny said. "We'll get old but we'll keep our bodies moving."

But now Franny had to wonder if they really would all end up old and happy and together. Jude's talk of dying had thrown cold water on that fantasy. And all that stuff about nursing homes, ick. Franny did agree on that. Communes, fine; nursing homes, no. And those retirement communities with advanced assisted living programs. No way. Talk about a slippery slope. From gated to dead. Blah food. Sad faces. Bus trips to smoky casinos.

CHAPTER FIFTEEN

JUDE PARKED IN FRONT of Anna's house and put her head down on the steering wheel. She ordered herself to keep it together today. She needed to back off the death talk and try for some normal time with her friends, stop with the Alzheimer's. And no more mention of killing herself which had clearly freaked out both Anna and Franny.

Normally she walked into Anna's house without knocking but this time she paused on the steps to put a smile on her face just as the front door was opened by an older woman in an aqua pantsuit with giant pink glasses. "How lovely," said the woman, grabbing Jude and kissing her on both cheeks and then pulling her to her flowery French smelling bosom. *Je Riviens*, thought Jude. Over the woman's shoulder Jude saw Anna hurrying to the door.

"Jude, you remember Rick's mother."

"Of course. How are you, Helen?"

Anna looked sharply at Jude as the older woman frowned and then laughed. "Oh Jude, you big tease. You remember I got rid of that old name eons ago. Heather, darling. Heather. And don't you look wonderful, Jude. I so admire your generation. You just go with your gray hair. So brave. So earth motherly."

Jude looked down at her big sweater, jeans and favorite red clogs. "That's me, a regular earth mother," she said, admiring Anna's short skirt and black tights and definitely not-gray hair.

"Well, you look very healthy and robust, Jude," said Heather.

Jude assumed she meant stout. "And you look very stylish, Heather. Very pastel."

"I know I'm rushing the season but I was just in a mood for light colors. California has such different rules. Back in Pennsylvania I never wore pastels until Memorial Day."

"And no white shoes after September," said Jude. "I grew up in Michigan. We had the same strange ideas." Good lord, how long was she going to have to keep up this fashion banter, thought Jude as Anna intervened.

"Jude, come help me finish making lunch. You can do the salad. Franny will be here soon. And Heather, we'll see you later. Give Nordstrom's our love."

Anna shut the door behind her mother-in-law and groaned. "Sorry Jude, the woman does go on with the girl talk. And you don't have to help me with anything. It's all done. Have a seat." She wrapped Jude in a long hug and pointed to a stool at the counter. "How you doing, sweetheart? I've been thinking about you a lot."

"I know. I mean, well, I assume you have. And Franny too. And I need to talk to you both about some of that stuff."

Anna widened her eyes and Jude said, "Let's wait for Franny." God, Jude thought, had she already blown it? What was that Heather thing? She saw the look Anna gave her. Okay, Jude had forgotten Anna's mother-in-law's silly new name, but she sure knew her perfume. Score one. Hadn't she'd read that people with Alzheimer's can start to lose their sense of smell? Well, hers seemed just fine.

Had she already said too much to Anna and Franny? Were they starting to look at her differently? She knew how a person's serious illness could change the way people acted. Friends put you in a new category. You became the sad, sick one, no longer a member of the club of healthy everyday people. Jude's sister Patsy called them "The poor dear people." Jude did not want to become a poor dear.

Jude looked around at Anna's blue and yellow kitchen, admiring the Provencal tablecloth on her long pine table and topped with a tall orange vase of purple tulips. How many times the three of them had taken over Anna's pretty kitchen, chopping vegetables, cooking pasta, cleaning up after book club, doing dishes. Anna's kitchen was almost as familiar as Jude's own, although something seemed different.

"Notice anything new?" asked Anna.

That was a relief, thought Jude. Something had changed, but what?

"Hmm, the cabinets?"

"No, my counters. Granite. Cost a fortune but I got a good commission on that Glen Ellen property," said Anna. "Insane prices, I know." She held up a finger. "Car door. Maybe our Franny's finally here."

Jude has seen her mother's old friends slip away. The afternoon bridge group kept her at their table for a while, helping her with her cards, but they eventually stopped inviting her. Jude had distanced herself from her mother, too. As her mother worsened Jude became embarrassed for her and by her. Became impatient with her. Even resented her for not being her smart mother, her real mother, anymore.

Franny galloped into Anna's kitchen in a purple poncho and matching beanie. "Do you guys realize it is raining? Come on. Let's do a little dance to the rain gods," she said, yanking Anna and Jude to their feet. And then they were outside on the brick patio, holding hands and kicking their feet like they were at a Greek wedding, shrieking, just like their silly happy usual selves, thought Jude. She twirled until she was dizzy.

Inside they sat in damp clothes, toweled off their hair. Anna poured wine. "I was going to do iced tea, but any rain demands a proper toast." She held out her glass and they clinked.

"Maybe this means our long drought years are over," said Franny.

"I wish," said Anna, "but I don't think this is much more than a sprinkle. Look, it's already stopped. We still have a huge problem."

"God, I know," said Jude. "I haven't taken a real bubble bath in weeks. I feel too guilty using all that water," she said. She reached across for the wine bottle.

Her friends were both staring at her. Now, why was that? Did they think what she said was weird? Did they worry she no longer bathed? Or were they just surprised to hear her say something that wasn't about wanting to kill herself?

"So, how goes it, Jude," asked Franny. She tilted her head in concern, just as Anna had done.

"Well," said Jude, drawing out the word. "I do have something

I want to tell you." She attempted a reassuring smile. Did they look frightened? Did they worry she was going to pull out a bag of pills right there?

Jude spread some brie on a slice of sourdough to give herself time and said, "I want to apologize. I know I have been scaring you two and I'm sorry. I do worry about things happening in my brain. But I decided I need to stop obsessing and wait a while, like Carly, my doctor, said, and then take some more tests." Did they look relieved? Did they believe her?

"Oh, thank God, Jude," sighed Franny.

"Darling Jude, you had us pretty scared," said Anna. She bit her lip and looked like she might cry. She and Franny stood up and bent over Jude to wrap themselves in an awkward three-person hug.

Franny sat back down and said, "I'm so relieved Jude." She paused like she was considering whether to say more. "Maybe you don't want to talk about it but I did want to tell you that I've been doing some research on you know, dementia, and there is this thing called mild cognitive impairment."

Anna put her hand on Franny's arm to interrupt. "Jude, is there something else?"

"Yeah. I think I'm going to give my notice at work. Retire. And see if that helps. And I think we should plan another getaway. And yes, Franny, I do know about mild cognitive." She hesitated before the last word.

"Impairment," said Franny.

Jude paused, and Anna practically growled to Franny. "Here Franny, have some more cheese."

Franny responded with a "what?" look and Jude continued.

"Some people maintain okay with it, the mild cognitive stuff, but it doesn't, like, go away. The word mild makes it sound a little more benign than it is. It would be nice if you could say, Sorry I've forgotten your name or in fact that I ever knew you at all but I seem to have caught a bit of impairment. Like it was a flu bug. And the other would say, "Oh yes, I had the same thing last week. Miserable stuff."

Jude laughed but her friends didn't. They looked uncomfortable, like they didn't know whether Jude was trying to be funny or not.

Or did they think she was being just plain morbid? Was she going to have to start editing her bad jokes, too? She and her sister used to call it their Alzheimer humor, and they got pretty good at it.

Often after Jude and her sister visited Ruthie at the nursing home they would go to a bar, talk about their mother's shitty disease and then tease each other that one of them would be next. "Uh oh, Jude, you already told me that story," Patsy would say with a devilish look. Or Jude would accuse Patsy of taking the wrong road. "Are you getting lost again, Sister?" It wasn't so much trying to amuse each other but to dare to laugh at the absurdity of what was happening to their mother, to push back at Alzheimer's, put it in its place and chase their own dread that it could be lurking in their genes, too. But the last time Jude tried kidding Patsy, her sister claimed she no longer worried about her brain getting soft. "I've decided if I don't have it by now, I'm not going to get it." That left Jude with no one to share her fears. She'd tried with her friends but now she needed to cool it.

"How about we eat?" said Anna, passing the salad.

"No quinoa?" Franny asked, feigning surprise.

"I've kind of lost my taste," said Anna. "The last office potluck was like a quinoa tasting. I mean how many things can you do with the stuff?"

"Are they all vegans?" said Franny, "or just painfully hip? Actually, I'm more of a couscous gal."

"Grain bloats me," said Jude.

Chapter Sixteen

"Have to pee," said Jude, after they finished lunch. She headed down the hall, pausing to look, as she always did, at the family photo lineup on the way to the bathroom. Rick's and Anna's wedding photo. With her dark eyes and straight hair, she looked like an Indian queen. A picture of Robby as a roly-poly kid in Cat in the Hat pajamas. Then the three of them, howling and collapsing into each other. Franny, head thrown back, snorted like she was gulping air. Jude exploded into her full-bodied roar. And Anna, the dainty laugher who made little puppy yelps, burrowed in Franny's shoulder. Happy people, innocent times.

She closed the door and started humming. There was nothing in Anna's fancy bathroom as simple as a medicine chest with a mirror on the front. Instead there were three antique mirrors arranged around a glass cabinet displaying pretty jars and artful stacks of little soaps, likely some Restoration Hardware version of a medicine chest. Very handsome but where do they keep the Band-Aids and all their pills?

Jude opened the small drawers in a side table. Nothing there but travel tubes of shampoo and a bag of throat lozenges. Of course, now that she thought about it, any serious drugs would be upstairs in Anna's and Rick's bathroom. Next time Jude would figure out a way to get up there. When Robby was still living at home there were no meds allowed anywhere in the house. But Robby was long out of the house, and by Anna's account, clean and sober. Hmm. Maybe Rick's mother had arrived with her own stash.

Jude had pretty much concluded that her way out was pills. Everything else was so grisly. She was too afraid of guns, didn't own one, wouldn't know how to fire one. She had to look away when she got a blood test, so slicing her wrists and sinking into a hot bath was out of the question. Hanging would be too awful. When Jude was little a friend of her parents from church hanged herself. The woman's daughters had found her in the attic. The kids were Jude's age, in grade school. Jude overheard her mother talking on the phone about "that poor woman" and "those poor girls" but she refused to answer any of Jude's questions so Jude conjured up her own horror scene. The girls probably came home from school, expecting their normal snack of crackers and peanut butter, and started calling for Mommy. Which one thought to look in the attic? Jude imagined their mother probably had worn a dress and heels. All the mothers wore dresses and heels back then. Would her shoes have dropped off as she hung there? What did she look like dead? For the rest of their lives did those girls still see their mother hanging there? Jude could never do that to Katy or Charlie.

Robin Williams hanged himself although it was more typical for celebrities to die from an overdose, like Phillip Seymour Hoffman. If you took too many pills people could never be sure if you meant to do it, which somehow made your death a little more mysterious and tragic. People were still speculating if Marilyn Monroe gulped those barbiturates on her own or if some high-profile lover had hired someone to make her death look like suicide.

You could Google all kinds of information about suicide. Before the internet you would have to poke in the library stacks for information on suicide and then risk having the librarian give you a concerned look and whisper to her friends that a certain woman on Elm Street might be having problems.

Their book club had gotten into talking about suicide after reading *The Bell Jar*. Sylvia Plath, head in the oven. Anne Sexton, asphyxiated in the garage. Ernest Hemingway, his favorite shotgun. Then there were all the famous dead characters. Poor drowned Ophelia. Emma Bovary with her bowl of arsenic. Anna Karenina on the train tracks.

Did any famous tortured women in literature kill herself because she thought she had dementia? No, most had a more romantic motive, caused by temporary madness and lost love. Those women also got to stylishly slip into oblivion, last seen in flowing hair and lavish dress. So much better to dress up for your finale, she thought, than waste away in some shapeless hospital gown.

Oh dear, how long had she been standing in Anna's bathroom obsessing over suicide? Her mind did that so much lately, starting out with one simple thought and then taking her on a long detour, until she finally stopped, like now. She studied herself in Anna's mirror. She didn't look like a demented woman. She smiled, stuck out her tongue and made funny faces. Then she switched on her Alzheimer's face. Mouth slack. Eyes hooded. Just like her mother's face at the end. She shuddered, shook her face back into a grin and returned to the kitchen where Anna and Franny were laughing.

"There you are," said Anna. "I thought you'd decided to finally get your bath, at my water meter's expense."

"What?" said Jude. She sat back down at the table.

"You know, use up our water ration," Anna chuckled.

"I don't get it," said Jude.

Franny leaned across the table, offered Jude the last piece of bread. "Jude, you were just saying you hadn't had a proper bath in weeks because of the drought."

"Oh yes, ha," Jude said. "No, I was just in there getting lost in all your mirrors, Anna. So, what's so funny?"

Anna began picking up plates and taking them to the sink. "Sex. I was asking Franny to tell me the latest with her and Tim." As soon as she said it, Anna froze and looked back at Franny. "Ooops."

"What are you talking about?" asked Jude. She gave a quick look to Franny. "You mean Tim, as in your ex-husband Tim? You're back in the sack with him?"

Franny fiddled with her necklace and felt her face flush. "I was going to tell you, Jude. I've been seeing a little bit of Tim. But purely for recreational purposes."

"How long?" demanded Jude.

"Off and on. Maybe a month or so." Franny gave Jude a sheepish smile.

"So why didn't you tell me?" Jude folded her arms and stared at Franny.

"Well, you never liked him, Jude," said Franny. "And it's not really going anywhere."

"But you didn't like him, either, Franny, as I recall," said Jude, aware of the edge in her voice. She felt hurt. Jealous. Franny had told Anna but not her. "Damn it," she said, feeling like she could cry. "Why wouldn't you tell me? Is it because I've become this weird fragile person?"

"Oh, Jude. Of course, not. It's not that big a deal. And I thought you'd get mad and tell me I was doing the wrong thing."

"It is a big deal, Franny. I want to know if my dear, old friend is having an affair with anyone, including her dumb ex-husband. And, no, I am not going to lecture you. If you want to sleep with the man who was a shithead to you go ahead." She sighed and wagged her finger. "Just don't fall for him again. You deserve more. You always have."

Franny took Jude's hand and squeezed. "Oh, sweetie, I'm sorry. It's just that I am really loving the sex. Tim is, at least, a known quality, shithead-ness and all. And I kind of like that he prefers me to his younger women."

Jude forced a smile and decided she better lighten up. She was starting to sound like a junior high school girl jilted by her best friend.

"I guess, too, I didn't want to tell you because of all you're dealing with," said Franny.

"That's my point," said Jude. "I don't want you guys to treat me any different. Because then I really would want to kill myself."

Franny and Anna both stared at her and Jude said, "Just kidding. But, seriously, even if I were losing it, I don't want to miss out on all the good gossip. Okay, now I want details. What is it that makes Mr. Shithead such a good lover?"

"Well," said Franny. "He used to be all slam-bam in the old days, but not anymore. He makes me dinner, plies me with wine, kisses me on the neck, tells me I'm beautiful. And he takes a nice long time, " she paused and smiled, "meeting my needs, as they say."

"I could use some more of my needs met," said Anna.

"Charlie is still a pretty good lover, I'll give him that," said Jude. In fact, Jude thought that if she could keep things normal in their love life, she might keep Charlie from worrying about her a little while longer. Several times recently when he'd asked her if she was feeling okay, she'd been able to distract him by saying, "You always make me feel more than okay," and leading him into the bedroom.

Chapter Seventeen

Jude couldn't let it go. Why had Franny confided in Anna and not her? The three had always shared everything about their lives, including so many secrets, promised to never reveal to anyone else, including husbands and kids.

Anna had said they would always be loyal friends "because we have the goods on each other." They knew that Charlie had a sometime email flirtation with an old high school girlfriend. That Rick had a taste for porn. They knew that Jude had a brief affair at a convention in Key West with a New York venture capitalist who turned out, via Franny's internet sleuthing, to actually run a chain of dry cleaners in West Virginia. They heard details of each one's first sexual experience, including Anna's with her high school science teacher. "I didn't even mind that his hands smelled of formaldehyde."

When Franny's father died and she stressed over speaking at his funeral Jude and Anna convinced her to stand up and tell the stories Franny had told them, how her father had taught her to swim and appreciate classical music and how he wouldn't let her park in his driveway because she had a Clinton bumper sticker.

With Anna and Jude in the front row of the church giving her thumbs up, she told the mourners, "My dad thought I'd gone to the dark side. But what he never knew was that Mom had long ago jumped ship, starting with voting for Kennedy."

They shared each other's dreams, nightmares, clothes and house keys. Franny showed Jude and Anna where she kept her journals and made them promise, "If I'm ever in a coma you have to go to my house and get rid of them before anyone finds them."

When Jude stopped dieting she gave Franny her size small Eileen Fisher clothes. Anna called Franny and Jude at three in the morning the second time Robby got arrested for drugs and they showed up at her front door in 30 minutes. Franny told Jude she was the perfect role model for older women—"cool, not cute." When Franny said she wanted a tattoo, Anna told her it was silly at her age, but drove her to San Francisco to have a dolphin inked onto her right shoulder.

"I don't know how women survive without each other," Jude said. "Men act like they don't need other men. Charlie says he only needs enough friends to carry his casket."

In Jude's mind, if she could still trust her mind anymore, the best death would be to have Anna and Jude with her. In one of her fantasies they would be at the lake and as the sun set she'd toss down her pills with some nice Pinot and she'd fade away as they took turns telling favorite memories. Like the time Anna got a fat commission on a wine country "starter castle" and flew them all to New York to see *The Producers* even though Anna didn't really like musicals, but she knew Jude had a Broadway crush on Nathan Lane.

Without her, Jude knew Anna and Franny would have each other. Franny always said the best thing about having two best friends is "I have a backup for my backup." Anna agreed, "Like having a best friend and a spare." And wouldn't it make it easier for Anna and Franny if after Jude died, they could say, "We were with Jude and she was laughing and she wasn't in pain. We held each other and said goodbye." Like in that Bette Midler movie where good friends go to a beach house and watch the sunset and then whoever was the sick one dies. Now Jude was really doing the pity pot. What were the chances for her to get an ending like that?

She was knocked out of her glum thoughts by Charlie barking, "Jesus, Mary and Joseph. Look at what Governor Moonbeam has done now." He threw down the newspaper, yanked off his ball cap and smacked it on the kitchen table. Jude wasn't surprised at the explosion. California would soon be getting an assisted dying law now that it had been signed by their Jesuit governor.

Jude and Charlie had long battled the subject. Charlie grew

up Catholic but was not a church regular, although both he and Jude liked the current pope. Jude and Charlie liked a lot of things—baseball, reading the Sunday paper in bed and going to sleep listening to jazz on the radio. Their politics mostly matched, although Jude was more public, in her *This is What a Feminist Looks Like* T-shirt. But on the issue of assisted dying they were unyielding opposites. Jude proclaimed it a choice. Charlie, a sin.

Charlie glared at Jude, daring her to spark them into battle but Jude didn't feel like fighting. She put two bagels in the toaster, squeezing her husband's shoulder in passing.

"Look at this headline," he said. "Right to die, it says. It's a right to kill. A right to give up. A right to play God. I'm glad I'm not a doctor. If someone asked me to sit there and help them die, I'd say, I quit. Get someone else." He furiously spread peanut butter on his bagel.

"Who's talking about being a doctor?" sang out a welcome voice as Katy walked into the kitchen, going to her mother for a hug and kissing her father on the cheek.

"Where did you come from, kid?" said Charlie, letting a grin reshape his grumpy face.

"Just in the nick of time," said Jude. "Your father and I were about to get a divorce over Jerry Brown."

"Oh, yeah. I heard it on the radio driving up from the city," said Katy, pouring herself coffee and opening the refrigerator. "No Half and Half?" Good news for us progressives, don't you think?" Katy said, making a face at her father.

"When you tell me you're coming, I buy Half and Half," said Jude to her daughter. "Otherwise it's too much on these hips," she said, admiring Katy's belted sweater and tight cuffed jeans. How did Jude manage to have a daughter with such a little middle?

Katy sat down across from her father and said, "May I?" turning the newspaper around and quickly reading the front-page story.

"Okay, Dad, what's not to like here? It says End of Life Option Act. Options, Dad. I'm not saying everyone who is sick should go ahead and pull the plug but what if a person is suffering horribly and they are going to die. Why can't they decide to hurry up the inevitable?"

"That is not for us to decide, Katy," he said "What if there were suddenly a cure for this horrible disease? What if they missed out on seeing their grandchild born? I know a guy from work. Grabbed his chest and went down on the golf course. Everyone thought he was a goner. He was pretty messed up for a while, but he came back."

"That's not the kind of thing we're talking about, Charlie," said Jude, unable to resist jumping in. "No one would hurry that guy's death. You have to be six months terminal. Two doctors have to agree. There are all kinds of safeguards. It will be done right. And now it can be done legally."

"Dad, even the California Medical Association stopped fighting it. The only opposition is the Catholic Church."

"And I'm with the church," said Charlie.

"What's Frank say about it?" asked Katy.

"The pope?" said Jude.

"Yeah," said Katy. "He's awesome. He even said women who had abortions could take communion."

"Pope Francis is not going to ever say it is our duty to help people kill themselves. Or their babies," said Charlie, pushing his chair back and standing up. "I'm going to the hardware store."

Katy pulled on his arm. "I love you but you're wrong," she said.

"And I love you too," he said. "And you're wrong."

They heard the door slam and Katy said to Jude. "I was going to ask Dad what if it were me? What if I was like the young woman, the one with brain cancer, who went to Oregon so she could die."

Jude shook her head. "I'd save that argument with him for a while, if I were you."

"But what if it were you, Mom?"

Jude knew that answer. Charlie would never help Jude die. Charlie believed in miracles. He also believed in the old let-nature-take-its-course thing. If Jude were sick and he couldn't take care of her he would, out of kindness, love and all the good reasons he could come up with, put her in some nursing home. He'd bought long term care insurance, "so when we're old and feeble, we'll get some place that will take care of us. We'll even have a patio so we can grow tomatoes in a pot."

She had protested. "I don't care how comfortable it is, count me out." But every month Charlie paid into what he called "Our happy hunting ground fund."

"What a waste of money," she'd said. "Let's just put it in our Hawaii fund. If one of us gets sick, we'll go find a nice volcano and when the time comes, we'll hold hands and jump in." Charlie hadn't even smiled at that idea, and now thinking about Charlie's image of their future, Jude imagined herself in a padded dementia unit with Charlie in an assisted living building next door tending his tomatoes and dutifully visiting her every day.

"I'm with you, Katy," said Jude, chewing on Charlie's cold bagel. "This law is a good one. It will give a lot of people comfort, just to know that they don't have to be in agony. You start to think about these things. There was a woman I knew in Marin. Remember when a bunch of us did that nude peace sign on the beach?"

Katy rolled her eyes. "How could I ever forget? You were all over CNN." She motioned for her mother to continue.

"Anyhow, she drove her car off Highway One, up near Jenner, and died. They learned later she had been diagnosed with something awful and debilitating. So, I guess she took care of herself while she could."

"Oh, that's an awful story, Mom," said Katy, shuddering.

Jude decided to change the subject. "So, how was that business trip to London. See any plays?"

"London? That was a long time ago, Mom."

Had it been so long, wondered Jude. "I guess we haven't talked for a while. So, what's the latest with the job?"

Katy got out two eggs, cracked them in a bowl and added water. "I've been thinking about poached eggs all the way up here," she said drizzling in vinegar and putting the bowl in the microwave.

Jude looked at her quizzically. "Vinegar?"

"Keeps the whites from floating like jellyfish."

How smart Katy was. The things she knew that Jude didn't know. Or did Jude know them once and forgotten?

"About the job, nothing new, but there is something," said Katy, sliding her eggs onto toast and smiling at her mother. "Or should I say somebody? I'm seeing a new guy. A doctor. "

"Really?" said Jude. "We could use one of those in the family."

"Actually, he's a resident. At UC Med Center. We've only seen each other a couple of times on real dates. I like him. You guys would like him, too."

"Oh Katy, this is lovely news," said Jude, hugging her. "You looked pretty happy when you walked in here this morning. And a doctor? Well, let's just hope your father doesn't grill him over how he feels about assisted suicide."

"Yeah, I can hear Dad saying, 'Well, my boy, what do you think about killing people?' She laughed. "I do think he—his name is Matt—could hold his own on matters of medical ethics. He's very smart. And kind."

"And?" pressed her mother.

"And interesting looking in a tall gangly skinny guy way. He even likes to dance."

"Oh, my heart," said Jude. "Then, grab him."

CHAPTER EIGHTEEN

"Hey, is this the guy from down the road," said Rick scanning the obituaries. Anna read the newspaper over his shoulder.

"Yes, the guy who walks by with his wife and dog," said Anna. "The people with the black poodle. And she, his wife, I assume it's his wife, always waves to me from their garden."

Anna thought about the neighbors as she cleaned up the kitchen. A middle-aged couple in the white house that was set far back from the road. It had a persimmon tree in front that every winter was loaded with scarlet fruit. Anna always wished she knew the owners well enough to ask if she could pick some of their persimmons rather than buying them at the farmer's market. But she never had.

The couple had been living on Anna and Rick's road for years. But neighbors there didn't really socialize, tending to prefer their privacy. There were no big neighborhood barbecues and about the only time people met was to discuss fixing the road which was really a private lane. The land had once been part of a huge chicken ranch divided into semi-rural one-acre pieces. Most of the residents were commuters who worked in nearby towns or San Francisco and could tell their city friends they lived in the country.

Anna sent flowers to the house and then on a whim decided to go to the neighbor's funeral which was at a nearby memorial park. There was a crematorium on the premises and she guessed most people who chose to use the facilities brought their dead ones home in a vase or planted their ashes in the ground in a tiny box. She wasn't sure how she felt about cremation.

The widow—Anna knew her name was Janice from the obituary—wore a maroon-colored pantsuit with gold jewelry and a striped scarf. She looked like a suburban bank officer, different from the woman Anna usually saw in jeans and a floppy hat, bent over her garden or walking their road. Janice, whose hair was short and dark, probably colored, stood at a podium and gave the eulogy for her husband. How brave, she was, to stand there, thought Anna, and not break down but speak of her husband almost like he was still alive, like she might later go home and say, "I was just talking about you."

Anna's eyes filled with tears as she listened to Janice telling about how she and her husband liked to have a drink together at the end of the day. Whoever got home first would greet the other in the garden with a glass of wine, sometimes a cocktail. "Jake was the better bartender," Janice said. "He liked doing fancy things with orange slices and bitters. Me, I'm a boring white wine person." Sometimes she said, with a sad smile, she'd drive the long way home just to give him time to get the drinks ready.

Not only did this story sadden Anna because the dead man sounded like a fun guy whom she would now never get to know, but his death meant the end of Janice being part of a couple, the end of a routine ritual that included a drink together at the end of the day. Anna couldn't imagine coming home to no Rick.

Anna had been the one with cancer, but she worried more about Rick dying than herself. True, he could brag that he aced his last treadmill test, but for many years he'd been a pack-a-day Marlboro man and had lately grown a belly that threatened to swallow his belt buckle. Why don't men worry about their stomachs like women, she wondered? When Rick's pants got too tight he bought bigger ones. When Anna's jeans got too tight she went on a crash diet.

As traumatized as Rick acted when Anna got breast cancer (enough to take a lover to feel better, Anna always footnoted in her mind) Rick was mostly fatalistic about his own mortality. "When your number's up, it's up" he'd say and relate stories about freakish deaths, like the man in Windsor who was killed by a fallen tree limb in his backyard.

"Listen to this," he'd said to Anna, reading from a newspaper report, taking ghoulish delight in the details. "Last week's wind storm had apparently weakened the limb which broke off just as Smith sat down in the sun with a beer. He died instantly."

"Poor fucker," Rick had added. "But not such a bad way to go."

Her husband might be casual about his death but not Anna. She could make herself sick with imaginings—getting a call from the CHP or the hospital, running to cradle Rick's lifeless body, then having to call Robby and then comfort her mother-in-law. Fortunately, her fears, which she allowed only rarely, would vanish as soon as Rick walked in the door or hauled his big belly into bed and said, "How about it, Toots?"

Years ago, Anna had begun the habit of white-lighting Rick to keep him safe. It started when she and Rick were planning a flight to London and Anna mentioned at a dinner party that sometimes she worried about flying. "I could white-light you," said the woman seated next to her at the table. Rick looked over at Anna and smirked at the woman in a long braid and Guatemalan blouse. She told Anna she would beam a halo around her and Rick, the whole airplane in fact. "It protects you from negative energy."

Rick laughed about it later, going on about "another Sonoma County shaman," but Anna argued it was no different than crossing herself, which she always did when she sat down in a plane. From then on when she and Rick flew he'd nudge her and whisper, "Did you white-light us?" He didn't know she did the same every time she watched him drive off from their house.

For days after the neighbor's funeral Anna kept an eye on the house down the road. When there were lights on, Anna assumed Janice was home safe inside with her dog. When the house was dark, Anna hoped that the woman had gone out with a friend, maybe to a movie. Or maybe she was inside, drinking wine, in her husband's favorite chair, wearing his sweater.

When Anna's grandfather died her grandmother packed all his clothes and took them to the Goodwill, but kept his slippers next to their bed, moved to her side. Anna teased her grandmother the first time she stopped by and caught her wearing her grandfather's cracked brown leather scuffs. They were much too big for her, her grandmother agreed, but she said she liked rubbing her bare feet against the bumps and grooves his skin had worn into the leather.

Anna heard of other people keeping an article of clothing from a dead person's closet, something that carried their scent. How long does a person's smell last in their clothes? Rick's would smell of green soap and wood smoke if he died in the winter. If he died in the summer they'd smell like the lake and fish guts.

On a cool late afternoon Anna went out to look at the reddening sky and spotted Janice walking by with her dog. She called out and asked her in for tea. "Or would you like a glass of wine?"

"I better have tea. Wine still makes me too weepy," Janice said, taking a seat on the porch.

"I'm sorry Rick and I didn't get to know your husband," said Anna. "He sounded like a great guy."

"Yeah, he was. Pretty great," said Janice, patting her dog who had stationed himself next to her chair. "We miss him, don't we?" Janice looked different, older maybe, from when Anna saw her at the funeral, her hair showing more gray, but attractive, probably close to Anna's age.

The women talked, mostly about gardens. Anna said how much she loved the stand of giant sunflowers that yearly flanked the front of Janice's house and confessed how she lusted after her persimmons.

"Please come pick some," said Janice. "We always have plenty." She stirred her tea. "They were Jake's favorites. I never could figure out how to eat them without puckering but Jake would dig into them like a bowl of ice cream."

They sat quietly and looked at the fading sunset. "Jake died of cancer," said Janice. "He was in a lot of pain but he went fast. I guess, as people like to tell you, that was a blessing. For him, at least. We didn't even need hospice. He just suddenly went."

Anna reached over and touched Janice's arm. Janice sighed. "You know a lot of my women friends don't seem to want to talk about Jake. They're either afraid they'll make me sad or sometimes I think they are afraid of it happening to them. It's like I've become their personal nightmare."

Anna, who had been about to admit she felt the same, checked herself and asked about Janice's family. She learned that Janice and Jake had each been married before, that they didn't have children but Jake had a daughter from a previous marriage and grandchildren. That family lived in Texas and had come for Jake's funeral but Janice said they didn't see much of each other.

Anna told Janice about Rick and their son Robby. "We wondered if you two had kids," said Janice. "I've seen your husband around. He's a nice-looking guy. And isn't there an older woman who I sometimes see coming down your drive? In a little green car?"

"That would be my mother-in-law, Heather. She lives with us."

"How lucky to have a mother who's still living," said Janice. "I envy you."

Chapter Nineteen

The rain fell in a soft, steady drip. This might even become a real storm, thought Jude, as she walked into the back yard with garden clippers. Now, what was she thinking needed to be pruned? Looking around and seeing nothing that called for her attention she set the clippers down and walked into the middle of the yard where the chaise lounge sat, unused for months, full of leaves and now getting slick with rain. Wouldn't it be fun, she thought, to just stretch out there in the rain. She kicked off her clogs, brushed off the leaves and lay back on the wet cushion. A little cold but not awful.

Too bad she and Charlie had never gotten a hot tub. But hot tubs were not Charlie's style. He'd worry too much about the neighbors catching sight of his bare butt. He didn't walk around naked even in front of Jude. Well, good thing she didn't have that hang-up, unzipping and wiggling out of her jeans.

Jude should probably be concerned right now that a neighbor might look over the fence and wonder what the hell she was doing. So what? She yanked off her sweatshirt before it could get soggy and settled back into the plastic cushion. Just for a little bit. She looked up at the rain and listened to the giddy finches and chickadees flitting from bushes to birdfeeder and to the rare sound of car tires swishing along a wet street. If the meter reader came walking into her back yard right now and saw Jude splayed there in her wet cotton underwear he wouldn't think, oh here's another drought—relieved rain worshipper. No, he'd probably think she had a screw loose, was off her rocker, crazy as a loon. But at this point maybe she wouldn't mind being a little bit crazy. Crazy is fixable.

When she was a kid in Michigan, Jude spent most winters cold, damp and happy. Her mother would scold, "Jude, you'll catch your death," and eventually order her inside. Jude would stand in the kitchen stiff and shivering, her skin red and raw as her mother peeled off her wool snow pants and jacket, stuck with clumps of snow, and draped the wet clothes over the floor heater. Jude still liked the smell of steaming wool.

When Jude's mother got sick she stopped noticing cold. And heat. In the winter she'd put on a short-sleeved shirt and sandals. In the summer, a wool sweater. It was as if her body thermostat was no longer speaking the right language to her brain. Even so, it took a very long time for Jude's mother to finally catch her death. Her death certificate said: Pneumonia and complications from Alzheimer's disease.

Jude shuddered and looked down at the goose bumps on her legs. At least her own body thermostat was still working. What would happen if she sat in the rain all day? Would she catch her death? Would that be so bad? When they put old Eskimos out on the ice do they die from the freezing air or the freezing water? How long does it take to die from exposure?

"Jude? What in the hell?" It was Franny, come to save Jude from herself.

"Oh, hi," said Jude sitting up. "I was hoping you weren't the meter reader."

"What? Seriously, Jude. You must be freezing. Can we please go inside? Where's a towel. Let me get you a towel." Franny started to run to the back door and then turned to make sure Jude was following. "Come on. You need to take a hot shower. I'll make us something hot. Didn't you get my text?"

"I guess not," said Jude, reluctantly standing up and following Franny inside. "Sorry, I haven't looked at my phone for a while. Since I quit work I'm not as much in demand." She saw Franny frowning at her. "Don't look at me like that, Franny. Last time it rained you made us dance in it."

"You're right," said Franny, stopping before adding, "But this is nuts."

Driving to Jude's, Franny had decided that if Jude wanted to know all about Franny's love life she was ready to tell her and was hoping for one of their old-time frank and cozy talks. Now she'd found her stretched out half naked in the rain and it looked like they were back to another strange day with Jude.

But, happily, Jude emerged from the bathroom dry, dressed and as much a mind-reader as ever. "Trouble with the ex?" Jude asked, stirring her tea as Franny pushed a plate of cookies toward her.

"Yum. Where did these come from?"

"Your cupboard," said Franny.

"Soooo?" Jude prompted.

"Okay," said Franny. "I know you never liked Tim, but he and I have had fun these last months. He's gotten a lot more interesting, more experimental I might add, since we were married. But as much as I like having an easily aroused hairy body to sleep with, I think it's time to break it off."

Jude nodded and Franny continued. "I've decided he's really not that nice a person. He talks about himself all the time. And I'm starting to feel bad about him cheating on his girlfriend."

Franny continued a list of complaints, ending with, "And he still talks with his mouth full."

Jude listened without comment and then said, "Well, okay. So, that's good. You're not thinking of marrying him again."

Franny gave her a horrified look and Jude added, "Because if you were going to tell me that, I was ready to lecture you like I would Katy, who, by the way, has a new boyfriend."

"You mean the intern?" asked Franny, relieved to have the focus off her. "Katy told me the other day."

"Where did you see Katy?" asked Jude.

"E-mail. I haven't actually seen her since we had lunch in the city."

Jude felt a little pang. "How long ago was that? My daughter never invites me into the city for lunch." She forced herself to joke. "I hope she didn't wait for you to pick up the check. She always does me."

Jude valued her daughter's closeness with both Franny and Anna. Her friends were better aunts to her daughter than Jude's own sister and Jude had always said, especially when Katy was younger, that if anything happened to her she knew Franny or Anna would take over. "If I'm not around, they'll at least make sure Katy gets to Paris."

But Katy had grown up and taken herself to Paris and Franny and Katy had developed their own adult friendship, independent of Jude, which made sense since both were single and occasionally got together for a concert or movie. So why now did that bother Jude? Stupid paranoia again. Katy would always be her daughter. Franny would always be her friend. And when Jude was no longer around, her daughter and her friends would have each other. Jude should be grateful.

Wondering why Jude had gone silent with Franny's mention of seeing Katy, Franny stood up and walked their tea dishes to the sink. She rinsed them off and put them in the dishwasher and restored the cookie box to Jude's cupboard.

"Well, I need to get moving," said Franny. "Have another boring meeting at school." She turned to Jude and wagged her finger, "Now, stay out of the rain, please."

Leaving Jude's, Franny thought about her email from Katy which not only included news about the man in her life, but Katy asking how Franny thought her mother was doing. Franny hadn't really answered Katy except to say she was hoping to see Jude soon. Today she might report that except for finding her mother sitting in her underwear in the rain, Franny thought Jude seemed to be more normal than she had been for a while. In fact, this had been a good Jude day compared to some others. Worth noting. Franny would write about it tonight in her journal. As Franny told her students, you never know in life what will turn into good material.

Chapter Twenty

Jude curled up in the wingback chair and stared out the rain-streaked window to the statuesque ferns next to the house, hardy drought survivors now finally getting to drink up. Jude, too, was thinking she'd had a pretty good day. Maybe she should soak in the rain more often. Might be just the thing for her. She'd tried most everything else.

"What's with all the kale," Charlie had complained after a week's run of kale chips, kale smoothies and kale frittata.

"It's supposed to be good for us," said Jude, who went on an anti-oxidant bender with each new brain food report. Broccoli, blueberries and walnuts, sardines, avocado and coconut oil, all said to be full of good stuff which might possibly stave off dementia, at least according to the claims of assorted experts and the marketing agents for the broccoli industry and all. And Jude, and the unwitting Charlie, gulped them down. Then there were all the exercises said to build a better brain. She walked most days, joined an aqua aerobics class that met in an outdoor pool at 8 o'clock, good grief, in the morning and amped up her yoga. Before going to bed she'd do a head stand in the living room, picturing the blood rushing into her poor addled brain.

Her phone went off, startling Jude. When did it get dark? Where was the darn phone? She followed the ringing to the coffee table.

"Hi darling," said Charlie. "Coming home. I'm bringing take-out. You want pizza or Indian?"

"Ooh, Indian," said Jude, gratefully. She hadn't given one thought to dinner and Indian food was loaded with that spice.

Bright orange. What was it?

Jude turned on lights and started to set the table, thinking how hard she worked to stay strong and healthy. But did anything work? Unlike a bicep, you couldn't see brain cells growing stronger. Or flabbier, for that matter. At this moment she felt okay. But her brain might jump the track tomorrow and she'd be burying a can of tuna in her sock drawer.

She opened a bottle of red wine. Maybe white was better with Indian food, but what the hell, red was, yet again, supposed to be good for the brain. It was a full-time job, monitoring herself, trying to figure out what to do, what to say, what to eat.

She had not gone back for another appointment with Carly. If she really was on the same dead-end route as her mother, Jude decided that the fewer people who suspected it the better. The internet was her confidante. It told her everything she needed to know about the enemy. Search Alzheimer's and up would pop the latest medication that might slow the progress of dementia, the best way to find a memory care facility, what your clogged brain might indicate if not Alzheimer's. Mercury poisoning, mad cow disease, stroke, some mysterious bladder condition. Ten ways to know if you have Alzheimer's. If anyone came across her Google searches they would know exactly what she was obsessing over and what she was thinking of doing about it.

She could give herself a high-five after the last online test. No, she didn't need help using the bathroom. Yes, she sometimes forgot appointments. Yes, she was often depressed. But not always. No, she had not gotten lost driving, except for last week when she was halfway down 101 and couldn't remember where she was heading. No, she did not have trouble balancing her checkbook. Must be an old test. How many people even used checkbooks anymore? Having answered yes to fewer than five questions, the computer assured her she needed no further assessment at this time.

But Jude knew different. To use a Charlie expression, it was time to shit or get off the pot. God, Charlie. How much did he suspect?

"You know what makes this so orange?" Jude asked as they finished the curry.

Charlie shrugged.

"Turmeric," she practically crowed, seizing the name of the spice.

"Don't tell me. It's good for us," said Charlie.

They were a pretty compatible pair, good old buddies, she and Charlie. Always had something to tell each other. This night they talked about the rain, could it mean the end of the drought? They talked about Charlie's lunch with the guys from work, and Charlie asked about Jude's day. She skipped the part about sitting in the rain and said, "Franny came over. We had tea."

She wished she didn't have to keep herself, her other terrified self, a secret from Charlie. It was like concealing an affair, editing yourself so that you didn't say something that would be a tip-off. When she found a story about Alzheimer's in the newspaper she would make sure he didn't see her reading it. If there was a character with dementia on TV she'd not comment. Did Charlie watch and think uh-oh? Did he worry about her? She tried to think how long he'd been bringing home take-out. More often than usual? Was it the kale kick or was it because he didn't trust her to cook? And he'd begun asking her at breakfast what she had planned for the day, where she was going. "Just curious," he would say, "now that you're in this new retired life."

Stop thinking, Jude. Back to the conversation. "Hey, how is George's father? Wasn't he really sick the last time you guys had lunch?"

"He died. Maybe I didn't tell you," said Charlie, tearing the last piece of naan in half and holding it out to Jude.

"George had moved him into their house, in the guest room. They brought in hospice. All the grandkids came. His father, he was a life-long Orange County Republican, kind of loosened up at the end, even smoked a little marijuana. You know, to relax, help the pain."

"And then he died right there, at George's?" asked Jude.

"Yep, but it took longer than he wanted. The old guy told George he had a dream of his dead wife, George's mother. He was at a train station and trying to get aboard and his wife opened the window from her compartment and said, 'Not yet, darling.'"

Jude started to tear up. "That is such a sweet story."

"Then what's making you cry, Jude?" asked Charlie. "You didn't even know George's father. And besides it was a good death. A nice ending."

"You're right. Lucky guy," said Jude.

Chapter Twenty-One

After her department meeting Franny walked over to the college library, a favorite sanctuary with its ornate light fixtures, sturdy oak tables and a rule about no cells. She spotted her friend Jeffrey's electric blue wheelchair at a back table. He looked up and waved, motioning her over. Probably wanted to gripe about the assisted dying law now that the governor had signed it. Well, it was the guy's passion, and he'd fought against it for so long. He would naturally be upset. She could allow him a rant.

"You okay, Jeffrey?" she asked, bending down to give him a hug.

"Yep. I know, everyone is feeling bad for me and my lost cause. But we kind of figured this would happen. The so-called death with dignity voices were a lot louder than ours."

"So, what will you do now?" asked Franny.

"Well, we can try to make sure that the law won't be abused. Thing still scares the hell out of me but I guess we must, as they say, move on." He grimaced. "I really hate that expression."

"Me too."

"But here's the thing. My friend's sister has cancer and he and his whole family are worried now that she'll give up, decide to end it. That's what I worry about, too, Franny. That sick people will think, 'Better get out of the way and die.'"

"I don't think that's going to happen. But there are so many people who are in such awful pain and…"

"Not to be rude, but believe me, Franny, I've heard all the arguments. But that's not why I wanted to talk to you." He grabbed her hand and said, "You like music?"

"Sure."

"Actually, I know you do. I remember watching you dance at one of those faculty parties."

"Must have been drunk," said Franny with a laugh.

"Nothing wrong with that," said Jeffrey. "You looked good dancing. Anyhow, you know I'm in a band, and this weekend we're playing at the Redwood Tavern, the old roadhouse off the freeway. They upgraded it. Basically, I think all they did was clean up the bathrooms. It's still pretty funky."

She snorted a laugh, causing people at the next table to look up. "Sorry," she said and softened her voice. "I know the place. Used to have karaoke. Jude and Anna and I got a little wild one night and belted out *Proud Mary*."

"So sorry to have missed that," laughed Jeffrey. "Anyhow, our band—we're kind of an old white guys garage band—will be there. We're trying to get a full house. I've been urging the kids, my students to come. But it would be nice to have some contemporaries, too. Think about it. It would be fun to see you there."

That Saturday Franny hurried from the cold damp night into the loud bar, feeling pretty hip in skinny jeans and black riding boots. She took a seat at the bar with a good view of the stage, ordered a local IPA and in a what-the-hell impulse added a shot of tequila and spotted Jeffrey in a black shirt with a scarf loosely wrapped around his neck. Very arty, thought Franny. The scarf was white with black musical notes. Jeffrey didn't seem the type who would buy something like that for himself. Maybe a gift from his girlfriend, the painter. Franny had looked around when she first walked in the bar and recognized a few people from the school but no curly-haired artist.

She liked sitting at the lively bar, even by herself. Not feeling awkwardly single like she might at other places. It was easy to feel part of a crowd when there was music happening. And hey, she was there as a groupie, seeing as how she knew the man with the fiddle now wheeling himself up a ramp to the stage. She could honestly say she didn't miss Tim. For two nights in a row she'd put Tim off. Too busy. "Really?' he said the first time.

Second time it was "Well, okay, then."

Franny waved at Jeffrey and lifted her glass of tequila. He gave her a salute. He looked good up on the little stage, bending into his violin, nuzzling it with his chin. This was a different Jeffrey. Well, well, Franny said to herself. She had another sip of tequila and began thinking how it would be to make love with a musician. Imagine what those nimble fingers and skilled hands could do. And had she ever noticed Jeffrey's muscular forearms? Come on, Franny, she chided herself. He's your friend and colleague. That could get messy. Of course, so could sleeping with your ex-husband. Anyhow, Jeffrey had a girlfriend, who Franny continued to look for but didn't seem to be anywhere in sight tonight.

Franny watched Jeffrey and his violin. He really made that violin hop to... what was that kind of music? Fast and giddy and sometimes one of the band singing out something in French. Then Jeffrey took over, holding one finger down on a string until it quivered and then whipping the bow back and forth to a high-pitched shriek. "Hoo hah, professor," someone yelled from the crowd as Franny let out a yelp and jumped to her feet, clapping.

At the end of the first set Franny walked over to him, still keeping an eye out for the girlfriend. "Wow, nicely done. I think I finally have found some country music I actually like," she said.

"It's not exactly country. It's folk. Cajun. Sort of. We do it all," said Jeffrey. "If there was a dance floor I could sit up here and play and watch you do your moves." He shook the scarf at her. "Like the look? Got it from one of the young geniuses," he said, waving over to a student.

"A new image for you," Franny said.

"Stick with me, kid, I'm full of surprises."

Franny suddenly felt shy. Maybe she'd had too much tequila. But damn, he looked good.

Jeffrey called the next day and thanked her for coming out. "Such a nasty night and there you were warming up the place."

"The music was great. You guys are so talented," said Franny, leaning back on her couch and stroking Oliver's hair. "You had an enthusiastic crowd. Too bad your girlfriend had to miss it."

"Well, the girlfriend is gone," said Jeffrey. "Shelly went up to Seattle to be part of a juried art show and fell in love with the place. She's moved there."

"That's too bad," said Franny, flashing a victory sign at her dog.

"We probably needed a break, anyhow," said Jeffrey, not sounding at all rejected. She always wanted to be part of an art colony. And she likes riding ferries."

Surprising herself, Franny blurted out. "You want to come to dinner some night?"

"You mean your house?"

"Well, yes," said Franny, now worried she had misread his interest.

"You have a ramp?"

Franny winced. Of course, she thought. Steps. Wheelchair. "A ramp? No. Well, let me think. Maybe I could..."

Jeffrey laughed. "It's fine. We'll have dinner. You come to my place. We can worry about fixing your place later."

Later? Pretty confident fiddle player, thought Franny, laughing to herself.

The next day Franny called Tim and told him she had met someone and didn't want to complicate things. "You and I need to end this affair or whatever it is we've been doing."

Tim was quiet and then said, "Well, I guess it was your turn to dump me. But if things don't work out with this new guy, I'm always willing to come warm your bed."

Chapter Twenty-Two

"Damn, damn." Jude heard Charlie shouting from the kitchen. Then, "Aiyee. Shit."

"What's wrong?" she yelled out, hurrying from the bedroom.

"Jesus, Jude, you left the fire under the tea kettle again. God damn it." She felt her face grow warm as Charlie hurled the kettle into the sink. He turned and glared at her.

"Did you burn yourself?" Jude asked.

"No, I didn't burn myself," he said evenly, "but you'll have to get another kettle for your tea. One with a very loud whistle, obviously."

"I didn't hear it, Charlie. I guess I had the door closed. Sorry."

"Yeah, I know, Jude. Sorry. Sorry. Sorry." He walked out of the kitchen.

She looked at the kettle. Poor thing, now dented on one side and burned black on the bottom. She'd put it in the recycle bin. But was that allowed? It was metal but there was plastic too. What were the recycling rules? Oh, shit. Had she really put the kettle on? Maybe she did it automatically without thinking. She often made tea in late afternoon. But actually, filling the kettle with water and turning on the stove? "I can't remember," she whispered out loud.

She'd also screwed up the night before. She and Charlie had gone to their favorite seafood restaurant and a woman walked in as they were getting up to leave. The woman greeted Jude effusively, even hugged her. Jude vaguely recognized the woman's face but not her name, and she couldn't think of where or how they might have known each other. Charlie stood there, looking from Jude to the woman and then held out his hand and introduced himself. The woman said her name, Lee or Linda, some "L" name, and how she knew Jude from when they were on the library board. Library board, good grief, that was eons ago, who remembered that far back, thought Jude? Anyhow, somehow it all worked, at least in Jude's mind, and they made some talk about the crab cakes and Jude and Charlie left.

Driving home Charlie had said, "Well, that was a little embarrassing."

"Sorry," she said. And then tried to make light of it. "Everyone forgets names. We should all have them tattooed on our forehead." But Jude worried. She seemed to be forgetting more names and faces. At the farmers' market she had greeted the green bean man. "Hi Gus, back again this season?" and then realized it wasn't the green bean man at all. Green beans weren't even in season. Oh dear, if this kept up she'd be hugging strangers and having them say, "Unhand me, Madam."

A bath, that's what she needed. In fact, that's what she'd been getting ready to do when the tea kettle burned up. Have a little tea, with maybe a shot of brandy. Oh shit, she thought, and quickly ran to the bathroom to make sure the tub wasn't overflowing. No, she was safe. Charlie probably couldn't handle a flooded bathroom.

Oh, Charlie, what was she going to do about her dear, sweet husband? They'd had their rocky times but she knew he cared and worried about her. Became frustrated with her. And now even worse, he was losing his temper with her. How much longer did she have before he dragged her off to some head doctor or told Katy they needed to do an intervention.

She dimmed the light over the tub, took off her clothes and slipped into the water. Maybe Charlie was testing her. If she were a paranoid person—and she did seem to be getting more paranoid—she might suspect him of trying to make her think she was losing her mind. Like that oily British actor who makes Ingrid Bergman come unhinged in that movie. What was it?

Oh damn, what was any movie? What was any name? See, now she had remembered old Ingrid's name but not the smiling Linda/Lee hugger at last night's restaurant. She soaped her arms. One thing about being fat, she didn't have scrawny arms like some of the skinny women at the gym. Her arms were fully packed but smooth.

Now, what was she just thinking? Oh yes, about Charlie trying to drive her crazy. That was silly. Charlie loved her, she knew that, and he would be furious at her if she killed herself. He'd feel guilty that he hadn't stopped her and, worse, that he didn't know what she was planning so he could try to stop her. He would be shocked and heartbroken and he'd be so miserable he'd forget to eat and go back to smoking Pall Malls or whatever he was smoking when they first met. She knew that. She felt bad about that. He would be wretched. She'd only seen her husband cry once and that was at his father's funeral where the piano player sang *Good Night Ladies*... whose idea was that? But Jude knew her husband would cry over her.

Was she protecting him by not telling him anything? Should she leave something to explain herself after she died? She would write him a letter explaining everything. No, maybe she would record something for him. He might be more understanding if he could hear her voice calmly talking to him. But that would also make him mad, because he wouldn't be able to argue with her or interrupt. Charlie liked having the last word and Jude usually gave it to him. They'd have a disagreement and she would think it was settled and the next morning he'd barge into the bathroom while she was taking a shower or look across the table and say, "One more thing." It had taken years but she had learned to let her husband have the final say. Then she would nod and he would sigh and it would be over.

All these things jumbling in her brain made her so nervous. She could go along for days and feel almost normal. She would begin to relax, to start to trust herself again and then something would happen and she'd be back up on a tightrope, looking down, terrified to slip and fall. She used to be such a confident person. What happened?

Focus, Jude. She slid down into the frothy bubbles that smelled like eucalyptus or rosemary, some kind of herbal concoction that promised soothing powers. She liked reading in her bath, with a cup of special chamomile tea. But ha, ha, no tea for you, Jude, today, and she'd left her book somewhere. She leaned back and stared at the ceiling.

She wished she could talk to her husband but she didn't dare.

He'd get in her way and she'd end up in some place like her mother. After she died, she could imagine how much Charlie would want to yell at her, that she had no right to leave him, to take her life, a mortal sin. She would surely go to hell and they'd never see each other again. She and Charlie hadn't really ever discussed heaven or hell. It was their deal. No religious talk. But she wondered if he believed all Catholics end up together. Jude didn't know what she believed. She kind of liked the idea of reincarnation but wasn't sure if suicide cut off your chances of coming back as anything you'd really want to be.

How easy, she thought, it is for religious people to have rules, to never doubt. Jude had gone to church when she was a kid, like everyone she knew in the 1950s in Michigan. Her parents were Presbyterians, members of the downtown old stone church, like their upwardly mobile friends. Jude and her friends went to Sunday night Presbyterian Youth meetings. They prayed, sang and smoked cigarettes in the alley.

Jude reached for the washcloth and scrubbed her face. She didn't want to think any more about hurting Charlie. He'd be okay eventually. He wouldn't be lonely for long. Jude read all the stories about senior newlyweds in the wedding section in *The Sunday Times*. She liked the ones where each had lost spouses and never expected to marry again. But then there they were, their old slap-happy faces in the newspaper, in love one more time, having resurrected a high school romance or recognizing they'd always had a soft spot for their neighbor. Jude had read about one widower who married his late wife's sister. The story said that he would continue to wear his original wedding band. His first wife had inscribed it with "Merely Love Her" from *Camelot*. Well, that did kind of make it easy to recycle.

Charlie would be a catch. A caring man, open-minded, except for the religion. Cute in a rumpled sort of way. One of her friends had told Jude that Charlie looked like Jeff Bridges. It was true, as a couple, Charlie had always been the better looking one.

Jude stretched out, pushing her toes to the end of the tub. She could use a pedicure but she'd never had a pedicure. Would Charlie the widower be attracted to a woman with groomed feet?

One night she and Anna had gotten stoned and come up with

candidates for their husbands to remarry if Anna and Jude were to die or get divorces. This woman, too soft. This one, too hard. Like Goldilocks checking out the beds. This one, too political. This one, too neurotic. Jude had thought of Kathy from their yoga class. She was younger than Jude, or maybe it was just the Botox. Would Charlie want someone younger? Maybe, but if she were too young she might not care to listen to his Vietnam war stories or sing along to his favorite Eagles. What if he started singing "It's a girl, my lord, in a flatbed Ford..." and the new younger woman just looked at him.

Anna had thought of a colleague who might suit Rick. She made more money than anyone else in Anna's real estate office. She could buy Rick a new boat. But Terri was pushy and might embarrass him. And she talked about herself all the time. Tell her you had a headache and she'd go on about her migraines. Plus, she would only go to restaurants with a Michelin rating. Wouldn't work in the long haul with Rick.

Jude had considered Alison from her office. She was divorced, had grown kids the same age as Katy and resembled that actress who played in *Field of Dreams*—athletic, loud laugh, no makeup. Peppy and fun. Next time around Charlie might want peppy. Also, Alison was a big Giants fan. Maybe Charlie would finally have someone who would go with him to spring training. Jude had refused to go to Arizona after that awful sheriff started locking up Mexican immigrants.

Jude poked at the bubbles and suddenly felt sad, thinking about another woman being more fun for Charlie than she was. She wished now she had a glass of wine. One Christmas Charlie and Katy had given her a bathtub tray. It came in a box that pictured a woman with her hair tied up in a ribbon, reclining in a heap of bubbles before a tray that held a glass of pink something and a bud vase. The tray came with a book stand and a mirror. Jude had tried plucking her eyebrows while sitting in the tub but the mirror steamed up. Where was that silly tray?

She looked down at her breasts peeking above the bubbles and thought that one good thing about dying now was that her body wouldn't get any older. She'd look okay dead. But really, she didn't want anyone looking at her dead and had filled out that form that said she wanted to be cremated. Where the hell was it?

Would Charlie love his new wife more than Jude? She would definitely be a wife, not a girlfriend. Charlie wouldn't just date. He'd want someone to live with. But would he compare her to Jude? And what if the other woman won? Do the dead get their feelings hurt? Charlie might argue that considering how Jude did herself in, all bets were off. Maybe his last word on this would be, "Jude, you don't get to be jealous."

She slipped under the water, her hair floating around her like seaweed. What was that movie where the gangster cut his wrists and drowned in the bathtub? She'd already decided she couldn't stand to cut herself. She came up for air and saw that the bubbles were gone and there was soap scum on the sides of the tub. The water was cold.

Chapter Twenty-Three

Anna looked out to see the brown UPS truck rumble up their drive and stop at their front door, closely followed by her mother-in-law's car. Heather got out, intercepted the driver and walked in with a small package.

"Look. It's from Tiffany's," Heather said, pulling a turquoise box from a padded envelope.

"How nice," said Anna. "For me?"

"No, darling, you don't need this, but one day, maybe," said Heather, pulling out a silver bracelet with one heart-shaped charm. "If I have to wear one of these things, I might as well do it in style."

Anna fingered the fine thin links of the bracelet. "Lovely." She looked at the charm. "What's this about?"

"I guess I didn't tell you." said Heather. "It's one of those medical alert things. The doctor advised I wear one after my last EKG, given my age and an annoying bit of angina. I'm sure I told Rick."

Of course, thought Anna, Rick would know and no, he hadn't told her. Anna was surprised that she felt left out and it must have showed on her face because Heather patted her arm. "Oh don't worry. I'm not going to die on you kids. Not yet, anyhow. It's just a precaution." She snapped the silver links around her wrist and held the bracelet up to the light. "All my friends back home are wearing them. It's the new bling. We used to all want diamond tennis bracelets. Now we've got something that tells the world we're fragile, handle with care."

Anna peered closer at the charm that had a delicate fleur de lis design and the word Angina. "And what's this? Rick's cell number." She looked up at her mother-in-law and said, "Very smart."

"I couldn't afford the 18-karat gold version. But the sterling's quite good, don't you think? It might be a bit grim to look at every day. Pretty, but a reminder of one's mortality." She sat down and put the top back on the empty box. "It's funny but you know I really can't imagine myself dead."

Anna gaped at her mother-in-law and then burst into laughter. "Oh God, Heather. You are something." As irritated as she could be by her mother-in-law's self-absorption and inane chatter, Anna did find her entertaining. "You want something to drink?" she asked. "I've invited the neighbor over. Janice, the one whose husband died. I've been wanting to get to know her."

Heather seemed surprised at the invitation. "Why, thank you. I do envy you your friends, Anna. I miss all my old gals back home. Husbands are wonderful and I miss my Bill every day, but I tell you, when you get to my age, it's the women in your life who hold you up. It's so much easier to handle getting older when your friends are going through the same damn things."

Anna hadn't thought about Heather being lonely. She tried to avoid thinking about her mother-in-law as much as possible. She was cordial to Heather and she tried not to resent that the older woman was sharing their space, but she had learned not to get emotionally involved with her. And Heather did respect Anna's and Rick's privacy. Since moving in, she had done her best to get involved outside of the house, taking a pottery class, joining the library book club, but Anna knew her mother-in-law had left behind a large group of lifetime friends in Pennsylvania.

And now she had this heart condition. Anna couldn't imagine Heather being sick. She was "a tough old bird" as Rick called her behind her back, and while she didn't appear fragile she was old, she would die one of these days and quite possibly in their house. Anna visualized a rented hospital bed in their living room, a frail Heather hooked up to an oxygen tank. The thought saddened Anna.

"What a sweet bouquet," said Heather, pointing to the yellow mustard that Anna had picked earlier. "Aren't they those wild things that grow along the road and in the grape vines?"

"Wild mustard."

"Now, who would think to put weeds in an elegant crystal vase? Aren't you clever? Is that a Waterford? Did I give you that?"

"You must have," said Anna. She'd actually found it at a flea market.

Heather shook her bracelet again. "Speaking of dying, I've been reading about those do-it-yourself funerals. Did the neighbor have one for her husband?"

"No, it was pretty traditional," said Anna. "And I doubt she will feel like talking about funerals right now," she added in a warning voice.

Heather kept on. "If you planned your own, you could make sure things were right. When my friend Elizabeth back home was dying she asked me if I would take care of the catering for her memorial. She expected a crowd of about 100."

"And you say California is weird," said Anna.

"I admit that at first I was surprised. But then I actually thought it was a good idea. I'm very good at planning parties. So, I called my long-time favorite caterer. Of course I couldn't give him a firm date but he was all for it. I thought something simple, platters of good cheeses and fruit, assorted beverages. But Elizabeth said no, she wanted a fancy luncheon spread and an open bar. For a while she called almost every day adding something to the menu."

"Maybe this could be a whole new sideline for you," kidded Anna.

"Actually, I think that's something I could do quite well," said Heather. "But you'd have to make sure you get a deposit." She looked over her glasses at Anna. "They'd have to pay up front. Of course, it was fine with Elizabeth. I knew her kids could cover the bill."

There was a knock and Anna went to the door. Janice's poodle ran in as Janice said, "I hope you don't mind I brought Missy. I don't normally bring her to people's houses without asking but she was whining at me."

Anna smiled weakly, but Heather clapped her hands and said, "I love dogs." Anna introduced the two women and went to the kitchen as Heather hugged and tickled the black furry creature.

She looked up at Janice and said, "I'm sorry for your loss. I'm a widow, too. As the kids say, it sucks, doesn't it?"

"Heather." Anna set the tea tray down hard and gave her mother-in-law a stern look.

"No that's fine," laughed Janice. "You're right, Heather. It does suck. Very much."

"Your husband sounded like a fine man. I read all about him in the paper." Janice smiled and stirred her tea as Heather continued. "I like these new kind of obits. They tell so much more about a person. You have to pay a lot for them, though, but I appreciate all the details. I read one where the man wanted his coffin draped in red velvet and escorted through town by white horses. Some rich winery fellow over in Napa."

Anna looked over at Janice who gave a wink as Heather continued. "He died of an aneurysm, after playing cribbage with his grandson."

She paused to take a slice of banana bread and Anna said to Janice, "Speaking of what's in the paper, did you read about the big flap over the new mini mall?" Janice asked for details and the two got into a discussion about local stores versus chains.

Eventually Heather retook the floor. "In the old days you had to read between the lines in an obituary to figure out how a person died. You know, if it said after a long illness it meant cancer. Brief illness? Heart attack or stroke. Died suddenly, probably suicide. If it was an accident they included more details."

She chewed slowly. "This is very nice bread, Anna. Anyhow, regarding accidents, that's what happened to my great aunt. She was killed on her way to a restaurant where all of us were waiting to surprise her on her birthday. I didn't like the plan but my cousins thought it would be so much fun. One of them took her to a movie while we all went to a steakhouse and waited. We were there a long time before someone let us know there had been an accident and Aunt Lou was dead, hit by a drunk driver. My cousin lived." She paused. "I hate surprise parties."

"Okay Heather, now that is enough of that," said Anna, checking to see if Janice was still smiling.

"Oh, I'm sorry," said Heather. "Am I being insensitive? I guess I find the subject fascinating even though it seems to offend most people. Maybe it's my new Tiffany bracelet." She squeezed herself next to Janice on the couch and held out her arm.

"I'll get some more hot water," said Anna, thinking she'd like to pour some on her dear mother-in-law's head.

When she came back into the living room Janice had maneuvered the conversation to gardening. Anna jumped in with a suggestion they soon plan a trip to a native plant nursery and finally Janice and her dog got up to leave. Heather embraced both and said, "I hope I wasn't too morbid."

"Not at all," said Janice. "I enjoyed our talk."

As the door closed Anna sank onto the couch and put her head back. "Good lord, Heather, what got into you? I said no death talk and that's all you talked about."

Heather didn't answer but walked over to the vase of mustard which had dropped a few petals. "Poor pretty things. They don't last very long, do they?"

Anna shook her head and Heather said she was going to her room to read. She was gone for only minutes when she came back in and said, "Just one more thing I wanted to tell you about Elizabeth. She died at home with her daughter right there. The daughter told us that she helped Elizabeth put on her favorite pajamas and gave her a cup of hot chocolate. Sometime later Elizabeth closed her eyes and died. I suspect there was something in that chocolate. And, oh yes, everyone enjoyed her funeral party."

Chapter Twenty-Four

"Wow. Look at him fly," said Jeffrey as a bicyclist streaked passed them downhill, hands lifted off his handlebars. "Jesus. Live bold, my friend."

Franny thought a careening bicyclist more reckless than daring but enjoyed Jeffrey's hoots of delight as he shifted the gears of his vintage Mustang on their way to the coast. She had come to appreciate the artistry of those hands even more since first admiring their fiddle-playing skill at the bar. She and Jeffrey were now a couple, with a wheelchair ramp built at Franny's front porch and new padding on her mattress. Oliver, stretched out in Jeffrey's back seat, had required no adjustments. The first time Jeffrey wheeled into Franny's living room Oliver walked over, sat and thumped his tail. The attraction was mutual. "Reminds me of Buddy, my first Canine Companion, another sweet boy," said Jeffrey, pulling Oliver's head into his lap.

It had surprised them both, this development from colleagues to lovers. Typically, Franny worried about becoming too happy. Tim and she hadn't worked out, not once but twice. It concerned her that Jeffrey seemed too casual when he talked about the end of his long, many years relationship with the painter girlfriend who moved to Seattle. He'd explained, "We just decided it was over, I guess." As to why they never married, he said, "Neither of us really wanted to make it permanent. We both liked our freedom." And then he'd hugged Franny and said, "And now I have you," which made Franny feel desired but not especially secure.

The weather forecast that morning was for one possible last

bit of rain which made Franny suggest they stay home, make soup and read in bed. But Jeffrey wanted to drive to his favorite spot on the coast and watch for a storm.

The soft hills that roll to the Pacific were washed and gleaming with every shade of possible drought-ending green. "This must be what Ireland looks like," said Franny.

"I love that country," said Jeffrey. "The music, the beer, the pub scene. People are so friendly. I was over there for a conference and ended up spending two hours in a pub talking to a bunch of guys. One of them came up to me, said he could tell I was an American by my accent and invited me to join their table. We got along like old friends. The beer helped, of course. Never mentioned me being in a chair. Or asked what I was doing in Ireland."

"I'd really like to get over there," said Franny. "There's a fiction writing retreat in Galway I've always thought sounded so cool."

"Then, we'll go," said Jeffrey, abruptly turning up a narrow country road lined with eucalyptus trees. "I didn't know you were such a daredevil," said Franny, peering into steep ravines as Jeffrey roared the car up sharp climbs and around narrow curves. "Who do you think you are? James Bond? You're as crazy as that bicyclist."

Eventually the road dipped down to meet the coastal highway. Jeffrey slowed and pulled into a parking area atop an ocean bluff.

"Whew," said Franny.

"Fun," said Jeffrey.

From their perch they could see a long stretch of rugged Sonoma coast with its sandy beaches and giant rocks looking like whale humps erupting from the ocean. Today, as promised, the ocean was churning and they could see a dark stampede of purple storm clouds heading their way.

"Come on, let's get out in it," said Jeffrey, reaching in the back seat for his wheelchair.

"It's going to rain any minute," protested Franny, reluctantly pushing open her door against a blast of wind and grabbing Oliver's leash.

"But it isn't yet," said Jeffrey, wheeling to the end of a path lined with succulent ice plant, dotted with tiny pink blossoms. "Isn't it fantastic," he yelled out, as the wind whipped his long gray hair back from his forehead.

Franny stood next to the car and held on to the whimpering Oliver who was begging to join Jeffrey. "No, Oliver," she ordered, imagining the worst, both dog and boyfriend plummeting over the precipice.

"Okay, now it really is raining," Franny said, grateful to feel the first sprinkles as they rushed to the safe, warm car.

"Ever seen the *Tempest*," asked Jeffrey. "I love any kind of wild, dramatic weather. Did I frighten you?"

"I don't like getting near edges," she said.

Down the beach she spotted a couple dashing back and forth into the surf. "People are so stupid," she said. "Every year people, mostly tourists, get sucked in by sneaker waves. Where do they think are, Santa Barbara in July?"

"Yeah, you have to be careful. Not turn your back on the ocean and all that," said Jeffrey. "But it can be so damned exciting to scare yourself. Go above your nerve. Isn't that what Emily Dickinson said?"

In the car they shared croissants and a thermos of coffee and Jeffrey recounted the many ways he liked scaring himself, including parasailing over Lake Tahoe and doing a zip line through the redwoods.

"I can't imagine doing either," said Franny. "I can't even get up the courage to go up in a hot air balloon, and every tourist in wine country does that. How do you do all those things?"

"Do you mean how or why? You mean because my legs don't work?"

"Well, no. Well, yes," Franny stumbled. "I guess that's what I mean."

"We gimps can do all kinds of things. It's called adaptive sports." He looked over and took her hand. "I think I've shown you a couple."

She put her head on his shoulder. "Yes, you have."

The sprinkles turned into a steady rain, blurring their view of the beach. "I hope that couple get back to their car without drowning," Franny said, thinking of a news story she'd been following in the paper.

"You know, there could be a body down there somewhere.

That doctor, the one who's been missing? They found his wallet and his car up the road from here, closer to Shell Beach. He just disappeared. Maybe the storm will wash the body up onshore. I wonder if he killed himself."

"Why would you think that?"

"Maybe he did something awful that he couldn't deal with, that he just couldn't live with."

"Well, that's a mood breaker," said Jeffrey. He straightened his body forcing Franny to sit up. "If he did kill himself, he was a coward. What about his family? Did he leave a note? Will they ever know what happened? It's cruel. It's always cruel."

Uh-oh, thought Franny. Dangerous territory, but she'd started it. "Maybe he thought he was sparing his family. Maybe he thought they would suffer more if he lived. Maybe he was sick with some awful disease."

"That's horseshit, Franny. It's always horseshit. It could be that he did something horrible. Something unforgivable, even. Or, okay, maybe he was sick. So now, does he get away scot-free?"

Hoping to calm him down, she said, "I'm not saying it was suicide. Maybe he was kidnapped. Or maybe he fell, slipped off the trail. These cliffs are always eroding. Two of those houses up the coast just collapsed and slid down to the beach last year."

"No, he didn't fall," said Jeffrey. "I've been reading about him, too. I read all those stories. And I agree. He probably did kill himself."

Oliver poked his nose between the front seats and Jeffrey gave him a reassuring pat on the head. After a while he said, "If you live in a body like mine you believe that you have to keep trying. You don't dare give up. And when someone else does, particularly someone whose body is whole, whose body works, when anybody like that gives up, it makes me furious."

He started the car and flicked on the windshield wipers. "Let's get out of here."

She sighed and touched his arm. "Wait a minute, Jeffrey. I need to tell you something. I've been thinking about this a lot and it's more than some stranger who may or may not have killed himself. There's someone I know. I have a friend," she started.

"She doesn't live here," she lied, and told him her friend was terrified of getting dementia like her mother and had said to Franny she would rather kill herself than live as her mother had.

Jeffrey listened, looking straight ahead, saying nothing. And so, as tenderly as she could, she told this lovely man she didn't want to lose, "You see Jeffrey, I think you might be wrong. It is not always a cowardly act. I think that the future is so terrifying for some people that ending your life seems the only choice. I think that is how my friend sees it."

She saw Jeffrey's face growing as dark as the clouds over them but she continued. "I think that in my friend's case she is not giving up on life, but believes the brave thing would be to end it while she can."

Jeffrey hit his fist on the steering wheel. "No, Franny, it is not brave to kill yourself. Living is what takes bravery." He backed the car around, turned on the radio and they rode back to her house in silence.

Chapter Twenty-Five

"Anyone have a special body part needing TLC this morning?" asked the yoga teacher, dimming the lights and clicking through her playlist. Franny unrolled her mat, sat cross-legged and waited to hear the usual complaints—tight shoulders, sore hips, the groaning chorus of back pain. Franny recognized the regulars, by face and malady. There was the sunny guy in brown T-shirt and gray sweatpants who had stenosis in his lower back and gave off the scent of a morning pot smoker. The brainy-looking woman who kept a *Wall Street Journal* stuck in the side of her gym bag and often came with one limb or another wrapped in an Ace bandage. Today the woman grumbled, "Everything" to the teacher's query of what hurt.

The class was a mix of shapes and sizes, mostly middle aged and older, including the teacher who was easily Medicare age and a plus size but who could bend over backwards and touch her head to the floor.

The early hour meant that most of the class showed up looking like they just woke up. Franny, who'd pulled on a green cami and striped yoga pants, found a spot next to a long body in baggy tights. It was the woman with the braid who did something in wine marketing and produced the deepest "Om" in the class.

When Franny was young only hippies did yoga, mostly as a spiritual practice. When she told her dad she was taking yoga he teased her. "Great, now I guess you'll want to move to India."

"Only after I learn to levitate," she'd said. Franny liked the way yoga moved her body. She also liked the darkened room, the Indian flute music and the bit of meditation at the end. But she suspected that her fellow yogis, like her, were there not so much to reach Nirvana but to keep their Boomer bodies as forever-youngish as possible.

The instructor called for a cat stretch and the class went down on their hands and knees just as the door opened and Jude walked in. She scurried to a corner, looked Franny's way and waved. This was a surprise. Jude hadn't been at Franny's yoga class for a long time, telling Franny she had switched to another studio closer to Sebastopol. Jude had a body similar to the teacher's, soft and supple, but now she just sat cross-legged and stared ahead. Was she meditating? Was she waiting to catch up with the class? Jude could do just about anything with her body, including boosting herself into a headstand while talking to you.

Amazing about bodies. How different each one was and what it could do. That made Franny think of Jeffrey. How frustrating it must be to have your brain say, "Move, leg" and have your leg go, "Huh?" His body didn't work automatically. He'd found ways to drive a car and please a lover. He could play the fiddle and make jokes and be the smartest person in the room, but most of the time he was stuck in a chair. He'd laughed the morning he saw Franny brushing her teeth with one leg propped on the bathroom counter and stretching. Now she wondered, did he resent her for being able to do that. She loved how he went all over her naked body with his lips and hands but how was that for him, to make her come alive in places that on his body had lost all feeling?

The teacher was saying something about staying in the moment but Franny was wandering on some dark worry star a million miles away. So many things can happen to people. She remembered her mom complaining when she developed arthritis that she could lift her arm only partially. She had to trade in her car for an automatic because it hurt to shift gears. "I've always had a stick shift," Mom wailed, as if it were the end of something. Would Franny get arthritis? Would she end up in a wheelchair?

"Normal is not a lifetime guarantee," Jeffrey liked to say. That sounded like a warning, a reminder to her and the rest of the non-disabled world they shouldn't be so smug about their perfectly functioning body. Could she ever talk to Jeffrey about this? It was pretty heavy stuff and so far they'd mostly just been having fun. Until that day at the beach when she brought up suicide and he went through the roof.

"Stay with the breath," said the teacher. Franny started counting her inhales and exhales but even breathing couldn't calm her flip-flopping mind. What if you couldn't breathe on your own? A friend's brother broke his neck swimming in Hawaii when a wave knocked him down on his head. Next thing, he was on a respirator.

Enough, Franny told herself, snapping to attention and joining the class on their bellies to arch into a cobra. And Jude? She was lifting her hips into a bridge. What was she doing? The woman with the braid looked over at Jude and then to Franny and raised an eyebrow. Franny gave her a weak smile. She didn't want people thinking Jude was being weird. But she was.

Well, this had been the most exhausting yoga class Franny had ever taken. Worry, worry. Jeffrey's body. Jude's head. The class lay down for the final corpse pose and Franny allowed herself one more peek at her friend. She was standing with one leg pressed into the other thigh, hands in prayer position. A perfectly balanced tree stance, but what the hell, Jude? Franny cringed as the teacher walked over and whispered to Jude who quickly sat down. Pretty soon Jude walked out the door, without even a Namaste, leaving her mat behind.

Chapter Twenty-Six

Franny started to call Jeffrey when she heard the text ping on her phone. Good, he must be wanting to talk, too, about their argument... well, his, more than hers... that day at the beach. But it was Anna's name that came up with the message. "Jude in accident think okay meet at Sutter."

"What?" Franny shouted. "Oh, no. Oh no, Jude." Okay, calm down, she thought to herself. You can't cry and drive. Sutter is not far, just off the freeway. Hold it together. Franny could feel her heart thumping as she circled the jammed hospital parking lot. Come on, come on. Let me in, people. A car backed out and she pulled in, coming to a jerky stop. All right now. No one's dead. But what happened?

Charlie was standing in the pariah area for smokers, away from the front door. As soon as he saw Franny he stubbed out his cigarette and went to hug her. "She ran off the road. Damn. She was conscious when the CHP got to her. But she was so out of it I don't think she even could tell them her name."

"How bad is she? Can I see her?" Franny asked.

"She's banged up but I think she'll be okay. Strong, tough gal, you know that." He took a breath and shook his head. "You go up. Anna's coming. I'm still trying to reach Katy."

Franny bound up the stairs, not waiting for the elevator. A nurse stopped her at the door of Jude's room.

"She's sleeping off the anesthetic but you can go in if you keep quiet. She should be starting to wake up soon."

"Why an anesthetic?"

"She broke her ankle."

Okay, ankle. Phew. That isn't so bad, Franny thought, as she studied her sleeping friend. Jude didn't look as awful as Franny had imagined on her race to get to the hospital. Her foot was elevated and sticking out from the blanket and there was a bandage on her right temple where Franny saw the purple sprouting of a large bruise. Franny had never seen Jude in a hospital bed before. She looked smaller than usual, like a little and older Jude.

Jude often complained that she was getting shorter. "I was always five eight," she'd said. "Now I'm five seven. Where did it go?"

"I think it goes into your feet," Anna had said. "I wore a size seven and a half shoe. Now I'm a nine."

What a silly thing to think about now even though she and Anna and Jude always compared each new surprising discovering in their changing bodies. But standing there in the hospital room looking at Jude Franny thought again that they might not get to become three old ladies in matching rockers drinking martinis. They could each end up somewhere different in an unfamiliar place, in a bed alone, wondering why their old friends weren't there to crawl in next to them.

Jude lay very still but she didn't look peaceful to Franny. Her mouth was moving like she was having a bad dream. Franny moved a chair close to the bed and stroked Jude's warm arm. Franny felt guilty. She was a bad friend. She should have gone after Jude the morning after yoga. She wanted to, intended to but had decided to give it some time and then call her. Admit it, she was more concerned with making up with Jeffrey. Franny wished Jude would open her eyes and say in her old kidding way, "Is this all I had to do? Get in a wreck so you'd come see me?"

Anna walked in. She'd been at work when Charlie called and was still wearing her Sunshine Realty blazer and name badge. She kissed Franny on the cheek, whispered, "I figured you'd need this" and handed her a cup of coffee. Seeing no other chair, she leaned against the wall by the window.

Jude wasn't asleep. She was trying to remember. That morning she had decided to take a drive along the Russian River. She hadn't been on River Road for some time and she liked the stillness of the water, especially in the fog. And there it was, sliding over the hills and slithering through the shiny green vineyards, come to float above the river like a white ribbon. Why did people complain about the fog, like it ruined their fun? They demanded heat and sunshine, but Jude appreciated a cozy foggy day. Sunny days were sometimes too much.

She passed a roadside cross decorated with plastic roses and daffodils. Who died there? A bicyclist? Drunk tourist? Maybe it was someone who suddenly decided to drive into the river and let the fog cover them like a soft blanket.

Now Jude opened her eyes to see a figure silhouetted by the window. Was it an angel? An angel might be nice.

"You're awake. Thank God, sweetie," said Anna moving to her bed.

Jude stared at her. Anna. It was Anna. "Where am I? Who put me here?"

"It's Sutter. You were in an accident, Jude. You broke your ankle and banged up your head."

"Ooh," winced Jude, trying to move her foot. "Sutter?"

"The hospital in Santa Rosa," said another voice. It was Franny, who appeared at the end of her bed. "You went off the road. You may have a small concussion."

Jude squeezed her eyes tight. "I can't think." She looked down at the thin green hospital gown, decorated with pastel squiggles. "Uck. It looks like...you know. What did our mothers and grandmothers used to wear?"

"A housedress?" said Anna.

"No, the other thing."

"An apron," said Franny.

Jude nodded and closed her eyes.

A nurse walked in. "How about you ladies wait outside while I check our patient and get her a little more comfortable. How are we doing, honey?"

Anna pointed down the hall so she and Franny could talk privately. "Charlie said the CHP found her in her car down a bank off River Road. She didn't have her seat belt on and apparently was thrown over to the passenger side when the car came to a stop. She must have hit her head on the door and they think her foot got caught under the brake pedal. I was thinking that probably saved her from breaking her neck or worse."

Franny touched Anna's arm and said, "But, wait. Why did she go off the road?"

"I don't know," said Anna. "An officer looked inside and saw her just lying there. When he tried to talk to her and said he was calling an ambulance, she became agitated and said she was late for lunch. She said her friends would be worried about her. When they put her in the ambulance, she demanded they take her home. She argued with them all the way here."

"That sounds like Jude," said Franny. "Who was she meeting for lunch? You?"

"No, it wasn't me," said Anna. "And apparently not you. Maybe no one. Charlie said when he got to the ER Jude looked at him like it was his fault. Then when he tried to comfort her she got pissed and told him she knew what he was up to. The doctor said she had a nasty cut on her head and was confused."

"Poor Charlie. Poor Jude," said Franny. "She must have really been out of it."

"Panicked, is what Charlie said. And I have to say he looked kind of panicky himself when he was telling me all this."

"I saw him smoking outside," said Franny.

"I forgot to tell you, Anna, but I saw Jude at yoga earlier this week. She was like in another world all through class. It was so odd. We'd be doing a cobra and she'd be doing a tree. Then she just left the class. I should have gone after her but I didn't. Now, this. I feel kind of shitty."

Anna squeezed Franny's shoulder. "I know. I haven't been around her too much lately. Work, home, husband, mother-in-law. I haven't even seen much of you, either, but I figure you're in good hands with Jeffrey."

They started back to the room and Anna said, "Maybe they'll keep her in here for a while and find out something. You know, do some tests. All these worries about her brain I think have been making her crazy, even though she says okay. Maybe this a good thing."

"Ever the optimist, my Anna," said Franny. "But I bet, knowing

Jude, she will blow this place as quickly as possible."

In her hospital bed Jude was already plotting. She needed to get home. She needed to get her brain to make sense. She needed to hold it together. What was that about concussion? She didn't want anyone making her stay long enough to look into her head.

She thought about her mother in the nursing home, in those early days when Ruthie still recognized Jude and her sister. After a visit the sisters would stand up to say their goodbyes and their mother would look around for her purse, the brown alligator bag that held an empty black wallet and one white lace hanky. Their mother would stand up too, tuck the purse under her arm and say "Okay girls, let's go."

No, no, no. That was not going to happen to Jude.

CHAPTER TWENTY-SEVEN

IT WAS A RELIEF to be home. Giants game on TV. A beer in her hand. Charlie in the kitchen making his cheese and green chili dip. Jude had been wheeled out of Sutter, giving the nurses a peace sign. Thank you, dears. Bye, bye. How gracious she could be. What she really felt was like their old dog Dolly, a quivering wreck every time they took her to the vet, just waiting to leap from the exam table, race through the lobby and claw at the door to get the hell out.

The hospital hadn't kept Jude long. She'd been able to make her break after lunch and before she had to watch one more numbing cooking show on the hospital TV. She got Charlie to stop for ice cream on the way home. "My mother always took me to the drug store for a cone after we went to the doctor's. Strawberry. Dr. McKeon. Funny, I don't even like strawberry anymore."

It was a simple fracture to her ankle the young woman doctor said. Won't take long to heal. Just stay off of it for three weeks and let that handsome husband wait on you, she said winking at Charlie. Jude put on her adoring wife smile and said, "Oh I'm sure he will." The challenge would be to keep him from hovering. She needed to ease that worried look off his face but she also needed time to think and make a plan.

Thankfully, Charlie had already given her a way to explain her accident. "What happened to make you run off the road, Jude," everyone asked, including the CHP officer who stopped by her room with an accident report. She didn't know the answer. All she remembered about that morning was that it was foggy and she was happy. Can you remember happiness without remembering why?

"I thought maybe a deer ran across the road," Charlie said to the officer.

Yes, that was it. A deer. Bless you Charlie, thought Jude, pushing herself off the pillow so she could address Charlie and the officer. "Of course. Now I do kind of remember a deer. You know how they are always running across the road and terrifying drivers, smashing into cars. The poor thing probably ran right in front of me to get from the woods to the river." The officer nodded and began writing and Jude relaxed into her pillow.

More luck, the hospital let her go without anyone ordering any special tests on her brain. A mild concussion, said the doctor. "For now, let's just keep an eye on it." That would play in her favor. No better excuse for an addled brain than a concussion. The mild kind. Nothing life threatening. Just an occasional slip into fuzziness. Yes, she promised the doctor she would watch for headaches and confusion. Hah. When wasn't she watching for confusion?

She sometimes tested herself. What did you read in the paper today? What did you eat for breakfast? What did you do for exercise? At the end of a good day she might give herself almost a B, on bad days, a D or worse. On good days she'd think, maybe I'm not so bat-shit after all. Why, just the other day she sang an entire Holly Near CD, keeping right up with, "We are a gentle angry people." Not bad. If she could dredge up all the words to protest songs, then something was working. But other days her brain felt like mush.

Oh yes, she had told the hospital nurse, she would of course contact her regular doctor when she got home. Follow up with her. Yes, tests perhaps. If necessary. Thank you again.

Sweet home, sweet living room, the late afternoon light making the walls buttery yellow, orange dahlias bobbing outside the window, the grandfather smell of pipe tobacco from the neighbor who sneaked behind his garage to smoke. Baseball.

Charlie scooped a corn chip into the runny dip, passed it to her and jumped up as the tall skinny guy hit the ball, rounded first, second and then slowed at third, looking around. The short guy with the gray sideburns between third base and home plate spun his arm like a windmill. Go, go, go. And waved tall and skinny home to score.

Charlie yelped with joy and Jude thought, "I wish I had a third base coach." She must have said it out loud.

"Uh, huh," said Charlie. "What? What did you say?"

"Oh nothing. I was just talking to myself about how helpful it would be if we all had a third base coach. You know, someone in life to say hold on or run like hell."

"Jude, you say the damndest things. The Giants are on fire and you're getting philosophical on me." He popped a beer. "Besides, you're not going anywhere, Dollface. Not with that boot on your foot."

How could you ever leave a man who called you Dollface, Jude thought? But yes, the boot. She had to stay put for at least three weeks. And then, what?

"Say, who were you meeting that day for lunch?" Charlie asked.

"What day?"

"The day of the accident."

"I wasn't meeting anyone."

"You told the EMT you were late for lunch with a friend."

"I did not. I did? Well, I don't know. I hit my head. I was probably thinking it was another day."

"Okay," said Charlie and went quiet. But not for long.

"And Jude, why were you yelling at me at the hospital? You didn't make any sense at all."

Charlie had taken his eyes off the game and was looking at her. What was this? He had her thinking all was okay, that she was home safe and sound. Now what was he doing? Was he interrogating her?

"Charlie, you're making my head hurt. Can't we just watch the game," she said, feeling a little panicky.

The phone rang and Charlie went into the kitchen to answer. Returning with another beer, he was back to being all smiles. "Good news. Katy's home from Mexico or wherever the heck she went. And she's coming up next week. With the doctor boyfriend."

Chapter Twenty-Eight

It was Charlie's idea to throw a small party. "Just a cookout. With a few people Katy told me she'd like to see. I think she's ready to show off Dr. Matt. She mentioned wanting to see Anna and Franny. You didn't tell me Franny also has a new boyfriend."

It was odd, Jude thought, that Katy would set something up with her dad instead of her but she could tell Charlie was eager.

"What do you think, Jude," he'd said. "We haven't had people over in a long time."

A day later he told her he ran into Anna at the grocery store and mentioned Katy's visit. "So, I invited her. And told her to bring Rick, too. You want to call and ask Franny?"

"No," said Jude. "You guys handle it. It's your party." That came out a little sharp, so she added, "Sounds good."

It bothered her, though. She should be relieved that she didn't have to do any party planning with a bad foot. But she had always been the social organizer. Did Charlie, did Katy, think she was no longer able? And a houseful of people was the last thing she wanted now. The accident had brought too much attention on her. But still, it was sweet of Charlie.

"All you have to do is take care of yourself," he'd said. "Everyone's bringing food and we'll all wait on you."

"I don't want to be waited on," said Jude. "I hate being waited on."

Then Charlie told her he was building a makeshift ramp for the front steps and she pounced on him. "That's ridiculous, Charlie. I don't need that. I'm not in a wheelchair. I have a dumb boot and it's temporary."

"It's not for you, Jude. It's for Franny's boyfriend. He has a wheelchair. Anna told me that. Or maybe Franny did when we talked on the phone."

"Oh, right, of course," said Jude, backing off. "That's nice, Charlie."

"By the way, Franny sounds smitten," said Charlie." She told me I'd like him, said we both drink Scotch. Have you met him?"

"Not officially," said Jude, trying to remember his name and what she knew about him. "All I can say is he's an improvement over that ex-husband she's been fooling around with."

"You mean Tim?" asked Charlie. "I didn't know Tim was back in her life."

"Well, he was, but no longer. This one has to be better," said Jude.

The day of the party the fog burned off by noon and the wind stayed down, delivering a rare near-balmy afternoon. Charlie, in his summertime uniform, khaki shorts, black socks and Birkenstocks, marinated chicken and set up a bar.

The first to arrive was Franny's boyfriend, who, with Charlie hovering, wheeled up and through the French doors and aimed for Jude, sitting on the living room couch. He maneuvered his way around her booted foot propped on an ottoman. Jude held out her hand. He shook it and then moved in to kiss her cheek.

"Jude, finally we meet," he said, taking off his sunglasses and smiling. "Franny talks so much about you. I'm Jeffrey."

Now she remembered his name. Jeffrey, Jeffrey. But what did he mean about Franny talking about her so much? What had Franny told him?

"She was so upset about your accident," he said. "How are you feeling?"

She didn't get a chance to answer as he turned away to wave at Franny who was coming in the door, silver and turquoise bracelets jingling. Franny passed a salad bowl to Charlie. "A new kind of Caesar, with kale."

"Ooh kale," said Charlie sending a smile to Jude and asking Jeffrey what he'd like to drink.

Franny's first words as she sat next to Jude were, "How are you feeling?" This was going to be the greeting of the day, thought Jude, who, if she answered honestly, would say, "I'm a nervous wreck. I don't want people asking me how I am and a bunch of questions. And I can't wait for you all to go home."

"Katy," shouted Franny, jumping up and rushing toward Jude's daughter who walked in with her tall skinny doctor boyfriend who held out two bottles of wine to Charlie. Now, what was his name? Began with an M. Matt. This name Jude was expected to know. Katy talked about him all the time and had showed her parents his photo. But this was his first appearance in Sebastopol. God, two new faces, two new names, two new boyfriends. Jude forced a smile and waved as she heard her daughter ask, "Where's Mom?"

"Over here," said Jude, holding out her arms. They hugged and Katy put her head on her mother's shoulder. Then she sat up and looked Jude over.

"Oh, poor Mom. Poor foot. I hate to see you like this, although you look a lot better than you sounded after the accident. How are you feeling?"

"As I told you it's only a small fracture," said Jude. "Don't make a big fuss. The doctor said three weeks with the damn boot and then I can move around. And because it's my left foot I'll also be able to drive."

Katy looked over at Franny who had planted herself on the other side of Jude. "Well, maybe you don't want to start driving in three weeks, Mom. Let's not rush it."

"That's right," agreed Franny. "There are a lot of attack deer out there."

"Ha, ha, Franny," said Jude. "Okay, maybe I won't drive right away but I'll be ready to get out of the house."

Katy reached across her mother to grab Franny's hand. "Mom, we'll be right back. Franny, you need to meet Matt."

Jude watched Katy do the introductions and Franny motion Jeffrey to join them. She heard Katy say to Matt, "This is Franny, my other mother." Looking to Jeffrey, Katy said, "And this must be the fiddle player." Obviously, Katy had been updated on Franny's love life.

Such nice and attractive people, thought Jude, looking around the room. Franny in an orange tunic with all her turquoise looked positively southwest. Katy's silky ice blue dress set off her long auburn curls. Jude was glad she'd made her own effort to put on cropped linen pants, the easiest to pull up over her boot, and one red sandal.

She watched Matt put his arm around Katy and Franny's hand graze Jeffrey's neck. Women look so juicy and alive when they're in love. Sex had something to do with it, certainly. She'd like to ask Franny sometime how you make love to someone in a wheelchair.

"Hey, Jude, sorry I'm late," said Anna, holding out a pie. "Peach. From my neighbor's backyard." Anna had been bringing dessert to events ever since Jude told her it was her penalty for always being late. "If we counted on you for appetizers the party would never get started."

Anna bent down for a hug and Jude looked up and said, "Thank you. I'm fine."

"What?" said Anna.

"I figured you were going to ask me how I was feeling. So, I thought I'd tell you the answer. I'm fine. Temporarily crippled but fine."

Anna winced, looking across the room at Jeffrey.

"Oh, shit. Sorry," said Jude. "That was stupid of me. Soooo, Anna, what's new with you? How are your fruits and vegetables? Have any tomatoes yet?"

Anna picked at her jeans and T-shirt. "You can see I ran out of time to change. I was gardening and then made the pie and then Rick and I got into it. He's not here. He said to tell you he's not feeling well because of his allergies."

"I didn't know he had allergies."

"He doesn't."

"What happened?"

"Aw, just having one of our down times. I'll put the pie in the kitchen and then find Katy. Can I bring you anything?"

"Maybe later," said Jude. She sat and watched as the party moved outside to the deck with Charlie at the barbecue and Katy, a brilliant blue dragonfly, flitting from guest to guest, waving her hands as she talked, reaching over to hug her father. It was like watching a movie with all your favorite actors. She could hear Katy talking about work, San Francisco, vacation. "We loved San Miguel," Katy told Anna and the two traded Mexico stories.

Then she moved over to Jeffrey and Matt, both looking serious and gesturing. "Don't tell me. Politics," said Katy.

Katy was as skilled at working a room as Jude was. Or used to be. Now Jude watched from the couch. Lovely group of people, she thought. These will be the same ones who come to my funeral.

Then Jeffrey was at her side offering to refill her glass from the bottle of wine he held between his legs. She drained her glass and held it out for more as he started in about a trip he and Franny were planning to Lake Tahoe. "I want to take her kayaking. She said she's never been." He looked across the room to where Franny stood talking with Anna. "There are so many places I want to go with that woman."

Jeffrey seemed like a good man, thought Jude, and a lot better for Franny than awful Tim. So why did she have to blurt out, "Well, you can't have her all to yourself. I need her too, you know." Where did that come from?

Jeffrey looked startled and then patted her hand. "I would never do that Jude. I know how much you mean to each other." Then he laughed, "Far be it from me to come between you powerful women."

Katy announced dinner and encouraged people to fill their plates. Franny delivered a plate to Jude. "You have to try my new salad. And this bread is from Jeffrey."

The party moved inside as it began to grow cool and Jude thought, okay, you can all leave now. Charlie had gotten raves for his spicy chicken, everyone had met and mingled. But no one seemed in a hurry to go. "My attendants," Jude said as Anna brought her pain pills and Franny helped her to the bathroom.

Katy sat down with two pieces of pie mounded with ice cream. "I think Matt likes Sebastopol," said Katy. "He hates the freezing summers in San Francisco and he's been wanting to get to know you and Dad. I showed him the garden and told him about how you and I used to put our sleeping bags on the deck and how you taught me all the constellations. I think he and I are going to try to come up more often, like every month."

Jude nodded and Katy continued. "And then we could show him more of Sonoma County." She paused and lowered her voice. "But, I mean it Mom, about the driving. Please don't for a while.

And will you keep watch on that concussion? Go see Dr. Carly."

"Okay, my darling, I will," said Jude. "But now I'm feeling tired."

"Of course you are," said Katy, motioning Matt over. "Mom's pooped and we have to get back to the city. I'll go tell Dad we're leaving."

It was hard work being on, editing herself. Jude had put on a good show but her head ached and her ankle was throbbing and she knew she'd been less than gracious to Jeffrey and how many others had she barked at. Now here came Matt looking like he wanted to say more than good night.

He slid next to her and said, "Sorry we didn't get to talk much today but your daughter says we'll be back soon."

"Yes, please do come back," said Jude, summoning a last bit of hospitality. "We'll look forward to it."

"About this ankle. I'd be careful and not rush into a lot of activity," he said, his observant doctor eyes staring at her. Katy says you're hard to keep in one place. Broken bones aren't my specialty. I'm in urology. But I know it can take bones a longer time to heal than most people think."

"Especially old bones," said Jude.

"Not what I meant at all." He squeezed her hand and stood. "I'll look forward to seeing you next time."

After Katy and Matt left, Charlie invited Jeffrey outside for a Scotch and Anna and Franny moved to the couch with Jude. Was this night never going to end?

"We've been thinking that when your foot is working again we should do one of our overnights," said Anna. "Not sure about the lake. Have to see how the boat is doing. But someplace," said Anna.

"Like the beach," said Franny. "We could rent a house for a night or two. One of those places on the cliff."

"I really hope we can go back to the lake," said Jude.

"One thing I wanted to ask you guys," said Anna. "Would it be okay if I invited Janice?" Seeing her friends' blank looks, she said. "My neighbor Janice. The one I told you about. My neighbor whose husband died. We've gotten friendly. She even enjoys my mother-in-law. I know she would really like a get-away and I've told her about our campouts at the lake."

Jude looked over at Franny, waiting for her to protest but instead Franny said, "Well, I guess that would be okay. Do you think she'd fit in?"

Jude felt her face grow hot. "I say no, Anna. We've had this newcomer argument before. Remember Franny, when you brought that teacher with the boom box. She got pissed when we asked her to turn it off and then all she talked about was herself, like we were her private therapy group."

"Oh yeah," said Franny, "she was not a good choice. But if Anna's neighbor is…"

"No," said Jude, trying to keep her voice low so Charlie and Jeffrey wouldn't hear from the kitchen. "The lake is our time together. Our special time. No strangers. Just the three of us. No extras."

Neither Franny nor Anna spoke as Jude tried to calm herself and sound reasonable. Why didn't they get it? "I'm glad you have a new friend, Anna. But the lake trip is just us. Why do you want to change it?"

"Well, let's think about it," said Franny. "Anna, you check on *Lucia* and see if she can still float and we'll come up with a date."

Franny started chewing on a fingernail, looked toward the kitchen and said, "I'm going to go help with the dishes."

"Damn it, Franny," said Jude. "Sit down and listen to me. I don't see why you guys would want to add someone else. Even if Anna's new friend is fabulous why does she have to come with us to the lake? Why change things now?"

Shit, thought Jude. The party was finally over and she had gotten through it, but now this. Franny looked at Anna and widened her eyes. Anna sighed and said, "Okay Jude. We'll stick to just us, keep to tradition."

That didn't really feel good either, thought Jude. Now they would be mad at her. Probably leave the party and go talk about her. "I'm sorry," she said. "I sound like such a selfish bitch. But it's been a hard year and I want to be with just my best friends. I don't feel like sharing. Maybe in the future Janice would work out just fine."

Like when I'm dead.

Chapter Twenty-Nine

"Guess where I went the other day?" said Franny as Anna wiped the morning dew from her porch table and set down steamy mugs of tea.

"You and Jeffrey?"

"No. With one of my students." She took a sip. "A death cafe."

"What the heck is that?"

"It's where you sit around and talk about dying."

"Sounds really cheery."

"Well, it actually was pretty interesting. I saw one of my students at a concert in Healdsburg. Nice kid. He wrote an essay for class about losing his mother when he was very young. He asked me if I remembered his story and then told me he'd been going to this death cafe and how it was making him feel better."

"But why would you want to go?"

"Well, to support him. He was so enthusiastic. And I think it's intriguing."

"You mean death? I thought it scared you. Now, it's intriguing?"

"Yeah. Think about all the debate over assisted suicide. Jeffrey and I go on and on arguing over it. Plus, there's all the memoirs about people's last thoughts on dying. And Sebastopol has death midwives and in Marin they're doing green burials."

Anna shrugged and Franny explained. "It's where bodies get wrapped up and put right into the dirt. No casket, no headstones."

Anna shook her head. "And now you're telling me we can go drink lattes and talk all afternoon about dying?"

Franny, enjoying her friend's displeasure, teased, "I tell you,

Anna, death is hot. It's the latest in pop culture."

"Oh great," Anna groaned. "Sounds as cold as ever to me. Gives me the creeps. You should go find Heather. She's in the house somewhere. She has no trouble talking about death."

"A lot of people don't, Anna. That's my point. People are so much more open about talking about death than they used to be. Actually, I've been playing around with a story idea, on how people like us, our generation, are planning on doing death differently."

"Well, I'm not there yet. I don't want to plan it and I don't want to do it. Besides, I don't think there are a lot of different ways, Franny. We will all die, pretty much like people always have."

"Not really, Anna. There are choices. Think about that young California woman with cancer who went to Oregon so she could take pills to die. That's how we finally got the law here. And then there's Jude."

"Jude? What about Jude? You're going to write about our friend in a book?"

"No, not about Jude exactly. But she gave me the idea. She was just so open about talking about dying and I thought there should be a book about this new preoccupation with death. Although, thank God, Jude's pretty much stopped her death talk, don't you think?"

"I hope so. I don't really know what's in her head these days."

The two went quiet. Then Franny brightened. "Anyhow, I thought a death cafe would be good research."

Anna took off her sunglasses and cleaned them with the bottom of her shirt. "Okay, I can tell you can't wait to tell me. What happens at a death café?"

"Michael, that's my student, began by telling about a dream he had of his mom. She touched his face and told him he was a good man. He said he could smell the cream she rubbed on her hands before bed. It was cool and creamy and smelled like roses."

"Do you believe it? That the dead come talk to us in a dream?" asked Anna.

"I believe him. I know that dream made him happy. He said he never got to talk about death with his mother. She got sick and then she was gone. After she died his father wouldn't allow any death talk either."

"My mother never came back to talk to me. So, you're saying everyone at this café sits around and tells sad stories that make each other cry?"

"Oh, Anna. Sometimes you are so close-minded." She sighed. "Listen to me. It was a nice honest conversation about different ideas on what happens after you die, what you wish could happen when you're dying. Some of it was funny. This one older guy, he had a ponytail and bike shorts, started in about the white light and the tunnel. You know, where some people think you are met by a person who died before. Heard of that one?"

"Seems farfetched to me. But go on."

"He said it better not be his first wife who shows up in that tunnel. He said, 'If I ever see that woman again I'll kill her.' Someone else popped up and said she'd spent all her life avoiding certain family members and she sure didn't want to spend eternity with them. Don't you think that's funny?"

"Hilarious. But, what did you talk about, Franny?"

"Well, the facilitator, younger than us and very friendly, told us right off that we didn't all have to talk. Just say our names. She didn't even ask us to hug the person next to us. But I suddenly wanted to talk about my dad. I said he was a pilot and I think he would have wanted to go down in his plane. That would have been my dad's way to die, I said, instead of living so long and desperately trying to breathe at the end. Then I started to cry."

Anna thought for a while. "That makes me think of that pilot in one of the books we read in book club. Where the author says the hero might have died two different ways. Either after a long life when he's old and sick. Or young in the war before most of his life can happen."

"You hated that book," said Franny.

"I wanted a clear ending. Not a multiple choice."

The screen door creaked open and Heather walked out, with a sunhat and walking stick. "Franny darling, it's been ages. What are you two talking about?"

"Fun with death," said Anna. "Franny went to a death cafe."

"Aren't they great?" said Heather. "Better than anything I ever heard in church on the subject."

"You went to one?" asked Anna. More surprises from her mother-in-law.

"Did they talk about the wish list for what you want when you die?" asked Heather. "I told them I don't care if this is California, there will be no smudging or chanting."

"We didn't get into that," said Franny. "But I understand needing to let people know what you want. What if you were taking your last breaths and someone put on some screeching opera and you really wanted Miles Davis?"

"You guys are weird," said Anna, shaking her head.

"I think it's important," said Heather. "I had a friend who asked her daughters to take some of her ashes to Nordstrom's. To the designer floor. She'd always wanted to shop there but couldn't afford it. She ended up in the pocket of an Armani jacket."

"You are making that up, Heather," said Anna.

"No, I'm not. The girls told me."

"Well then, Franny, here's the person who should be in your death book."

"Really, Franny? I'd love to be in a book," said Heather.

"I'm not necessarily writing any book, Heather. But Anna's right, you would be perfect. You have a healthy progressive attitude about death."

"Might as well," said Heather. "Now I'm going for a walk," patting Anna's knee in a rare affectionate gesture and starting down the steps.

They watched the older woman walk to the road. "She's a hoot," said Franny.

"Yes, she really is. I guess we're settling in. I'm starting to almost like her again."

Franny pointed to Anna's front yard. "Look, your Naked Ladies are starting to show their little pink heads." Anna's garden was a country scramble of flowers and vegetables, the opposite of Franny's orderly urban garden.

"Those are your bulbs, Franny. I dug them up from your yard years ago. I call them my Franny flowers. I like having plants with ancestry. But aren't they early?"

"Yes, like everything else this year. I love them too. But that means another summer coming to an end."

"School shouldn't start in August," said Anna. "Poor kids going back to school when they should still be running through sprinklers. I personally need more summer, which, as I recall, was what we were supposed to be talking about this morning. Going to the lake. A lot more fun than a death cafe."

"What about the boat?"

"Rick says *Lucia* will be fine. He's been off fishing with his friends and said the boat was running okay. So, it's a go."

Anna leaned forward in her chair and waved. "There's Janice, out with her dog." She hollered out, "Hey, Janice, come on up."

"Speaking of," said Franny, "What did you think about Jude flipping out over your idea to ask Janice."

"I guess I get it. But to tell you the truth, I'm kind of weary of Jude's moodiness. She gets us worrying about her, like you said, that she wants to die. Then she gets in the accident and we rush to her bedside and she's out of it. But then she's okay and running the show again. I never know which Jude I'm going to get."

"I get that," said Franny, surprised at how annoyed Anna sounded. "But I understand her wanting the lake to be just us. We are a threesome. Just like you said about those flowers. We belong to each other."

She was relieved to see Anna nodding her head.

"And right now," said Franny, "Jude seems to need us, you and me, maybe more than we need her, which is different. Jeffrey told me that Jude practically bit his head off at the party. She told Jeffrey he was taking up too much of my time. That made me feel guilty that we'd left her on the couch by herself while we all chatted."

"That's what I mean," said Anna. "We're all tiptoeing around Jude. I thought she seemed to be enjoying herself at her little party. Until she took my head off, too. Sometimes I don't know whether to sympathize or tell her to snap out of it. "

She looked at Franny. "Of course, I wouldn't say that to her. She makes me crazy but I love her. And I worry about her. There is a sadness about our Jude."

Franny watched Janice stride up the drive. Long legs, burgundy hiking shorts, pale gray safari hat. "Very REI," said Franny. "Did you tell her about the lake? Had you already invited her when you asked us?"

"No, of course not," said Anna. "Okay, I hinted, but I didn't invite her. I said maybe sometime she could join us. I did tell her after the party that we had decided this time it would be just us three. Maybe another year she could come. She was cool with it."

"Hmm," said Franny, feeling some of Jude's jealousy over Anna's new friend.

"She's a wonderful woman," said Anna. "I feel comfortable with her. I feel like I can tell her anything."

"You can tell me anything, Anna," said Franny.

"Of course. But she's practically right next door. We can have a glass of wine and talk every day if we want. Maybe it's like you and Jeffrey. Someone new comes into your life and there's an immediate bond, a kind of intimacy. With you and Jeffrey there's romance, too, but something like that happens with friends too, don't you think? It's encouraging, really. That you can be as old as we are and still meet someone special?"

"Hello," said Janice, setting a basket of peaches on the step. She kissed Anna on the cheek and held out her hand. "I'm Janice. Which one are you? Franny or Jude?"

Chapter Thirty

Franny argued with herself all the way home. Really, what was so awful about a book on dying? Anna had just plain overreacted when Franny brought it up. Anna was so squeamish. That was her problem. But why get on Franny for wanting to write about it?

Franny played with the car radio. Right now, she could use the steady intelligent voice of Terry Gross, but Terry was over. She tried the classical station but it was on a Wagnerian kick. Maybe some righteous raging from Berkeley radio. No, she needed quiet to think.

Traffic slowed and stopped. Of course, the 101 was always clogged. So she sat and waited, stared up at a feathery line of eucalyptus on the hill and scolded herself. Face it, Franny, Anna wasn't upset about you writing about death cafes or death midwives even though she clearly doesn't think much of either. It was all about Jude.

Franny replayed Anna's accusing voice, "So you're going to write about our friend? Tell the world about Jude?" Damn Anna for calling her on what Franny was precisely planning to do—write about one woman's fixation on death and her quandary over whether to kill herself to escape an awful disease.

But, it would be a novel. Franny wouldn't call her character Jude. People wouldn't assume that she was writing about a real person.

Well, that was bullshit, Franny. Of course, some people, any of Jude's friends or family, could make the connection. Yeah, but didn't everyone worry about getting old and their brains turning to oatmeal? Jude wasn't the only one.

Franny hadn't thought of turning her notes into anything more when she began filling her journal with Jude. She was trying to sort out her own worries over Jude. Any kind of death talk used to scare her but now she was fascinated. Everybody seemed to be writing about it. Mothers dying, husbands dying, dogs dying. There was that book by what's-her-name, one of the many young famous super successful women writers more talented than Franny could ever hope to be. About a dying friend. She could Google the name, but she couldn't risk another ticket for using her phone while driving. Really, she understood the law, but why wasn't it okay to use your phone when you're not even moving?

Anna made her feel like she was some sort of ghoul, but face it, Franny had some of same qualms. Was she going to exploit a friend? Anna had eventually let Franny change the subject. But Franny still felt crummy.

Was it okay to write about someone else's life? Jude had confided in Franny and Anna because she trusted them. She counted on them to not tell anyone, not even Charlie or Katy. And here was Franny secretly recording Jude's anguish. Writing things down like, "I don't want to lose myself." And Jude vowing to never end up like Ruthie, stuck in a nursing home, wearing "some dead woman's ugly yellow sweater."

Jude might someday make a sad and powerful story. But why should Franny get to take Jude's words? They belonged to Jude. But Jude would never use them. Jude wasn't a writer. Jude was a social worker with a big, fat kind heart who spent her career helping terrified women leave their abusers. Maybe Franny should simply tell Jude. Tell her she wanted to write about her. And Jude might think it was fine. She might say, "Sure, Franny, take my life, write a best seller. Just change my name and while you're at it make me a Palomino blonde and describe me as svelte."

Jude had always been Franny's champion, raving over each short story Franny sent to magazines, and then after she got a rejection letter, which was most of the time, Jude would urge her on. "You've got talent, Franny. It'll happen for you." She promised that when Franny wrote her great American novel, Jude and Anna would put on a book launch party. "We'll make all the food and bring wine and Anna and I will be in the audience and ask you smart questions for which you'll have clever answers. We'll practice. Then we'll sit at your side and keep your glass full while you sign piles of books."

That was the old Jude talking. The new Jude was unpredictable. If Franny asked if she could write about her she didn't know how Jude would respond.

Stop it, she told herself. She flipped up her visor mirror and studied her teeth. She spotted some chin hairs. She kept tweezers and dental floss in the storage box between the front seats for just such emergencies. What was it Anna called the face fuzz? Billy goat chin. Franny started to laugh just as a car horn blasted behind her. She turned to see the driver scowl and wave her forward. Traffic was moving.

When she got home, Jeffrey was chopping vegetables in the kitchen. She told him her traffic woes and he told her to sit and let him make dinner. "You are a beautiful man," she said, thinking how cozy they had become with each other.

He passed her a slice of red pepper and she said, "Can I ask you something?"

"Shoot."

"Do you think it's all right for a writer to use another person's life in a novel?"

"Uh, oh. You writing about me?"

"Not yet. I still have much more to learn about you," Franny said, walking over for a kiss.

"Well, who then?"

"Not anyone in particular. I was just thinking. It often comes up in class.

"Everyone in there thinks they have a novel in them. Well, who doesn't? I do, too. And so many famous writers say write what you know. I'm just not sure it extends to who you know. How far can you go with someone else's life?"

"What was it Nora Ephron said, that everything is copy?" said Jeffrey, holding a loaf of seeded sour dough and rummaging through Franny's knife drawer.

"Don't cut yourself," she said, reaching over for a bread knife. "Yeah, you're right."

"Well, there you go," said Jeffrey. "Nora Ephron wrote about everything and everyone in her life."

"It's true, she did," said Franny. "The only thing she didn't write about was when she knew she was dying."

Chapter Thirty-One

Anna put on her dark glasses and settled in to people-watch. The flight from San Diego to San Francisco was delayed so she had time for her favorite airport sport. Travelers were so preoccupied they didn't even notice someone staring at them. Anna studied couples. Were they long-time marrieds or new lovers? Were they affectionate? Bored? Who was the boss? Who touched? Who talked?

Here was a pair, looked to be in their 60s, same as her and Rick. He was reading the *Times* and she was knitting something pale green. Anna had knitted one year to keep herself from snacking. Lost 10 pounds and everyone on her Christmas list got a mohair scarf. Was the knitter, glasses perched on nose, feet clad in spongy Mary Janes, making some tiny thing for a grandchild they were off to meet for the first time?

Anna wondered if having grandchildren helped a marriage. Gave a couple someone new to share, to be part of a child's future. She and Rick would make fun grandparents, certainly indulgent, the way they both liked to spend money.

But Robby might worry about passing on addictive genes. She and Rick had agonized for a long time over how much of Robby's nightmare was their fault. Was there anything they might have done to save him from screwing up his life with drugs? He'd started smoking pot in high school and then before they knew it he moved into the nasty stuff. Then, problems at school. Terrible, tearful fights with Rick and Anna. Counselors and therapy and finally an intervention to get him into the first of three residential treatment centers to take on his demons. Now, they didn't see him much. He was finally clean and living in Colorado, but didn't seem interested in returning to California or sharing any details of his life, at least not with his parents.

Every teenager smoked pot in the 80s, and most of their parents, including Anna and Rick. Anna had confessed in family therapy that getting high like her son and his teenage friends made her feel like "we were the super cool parents." Rick had given up pot but Anna hadn't. Franny had once gotten into Anna's car and waved at the air. "Good lord. Did the Grateful Dead spend the night in here?" After that Anna bought a second Lexus for driving her real estate clients. Wine Country might be turning into Weed Country, but one couldn't assume everyone indulged.

She looked over at the couple by the window. Late 40s, stylish, definitely extra-leg-room types, with their creamy leather carry-ons, her spiky gold sandals and his linen jacket. Both were reading. She had a Louise Penny paperback. He stared into an iPad. One problem with iPads, you could never tell what people were reading. But whatever it was, the guy was grinning. Maybe some of Rick's porn.

It was entertaining to consider other people's relationships, even though you couldn't tell much about the state of a marriage just by observing a couple. As her Aunt Jane used to say, "You don't sleep under their bed."

Anna and Rick might appear compatible but not like in the early years when people would speak of them in one word, *RickandAnna*. That had changed after his affair although even today their friends might still describe them as happy. Or happy enough. Anna would call them so-so happy. They still said "Love you" on occasion in a have-a-nice-day kind of way but their marriage didn't have much sizzle. Of course, they'd been married for more than 40 years. What more could you expect? Actually, Anna wanted more of something. The last time she and Janice split a bottle of wine Janice asked if she'd ever gone out on Rick. "No," said Anna, adding, "Not yet." She held that one in her back pocket. Her group-on for one retaliatory affair.

Now, that laughing couple just walking up was still dressed for sunny San Diego. His shirt was decorated with sailboats, and were those Topsiders? The woman, in a long white dress, reached into a bag and pulled out a piece of croissant and held it to his lips. Nothing like vacation sex, thought Anna. The woman reminded her a little of Janice who would look lovely and willowy in a gauzy sundress.

Over there was an indignant traveler. A pony-tailed woman with a travel pillow coiled around her neck glowered at a little kid with a chocolate donut who was perched on his mother's lap. Ms. Ponytail looked like she wanted to walk over and scrub that cute face with a wet wipe. Instead she got up and stomped to the counter to apparently demand reasons for the delay, then returned to grouse to her male companion who said nothing. A Mr. Whatever. Anna knew those kinds of couples, the ones people describe as, "She's difficult but he's so nice." Maybe or maybe not. Mr. Whatever can also be passive aggressive, happy to let his wife play the bitch.

Anna decided if the plane didn't leave soon, she'd get a Bloody Mary. The business trip had reminded her how much she enjoyed traveling by herself. No husband. No one else to worry about.

But this time she'd only been away four days. What if she were suddenly permanently on her own? When she was younger, she fantasized about leaving it all, family, house, job, and taking off. A favorite fantasy was having sex with a stranger on a train. Pulling off each other's clothes as the train rocked and clanged through some dark foreign countryside, making Italian love. Was that in an Erica Jong novel? Or a movie? She laughed to herself. Who would want to make a movie of an aging realtor in a ho-hum marriage looking for a roll in the upper berth? One of Anna's favorite starting-over films was *An Unmarried Woman* with Jill Clayburgh—dumped by her unfaithful husband to then find yummy Alan Bates. Anna was a lot older now than Jill Clayburgh's character. Damn, poor Jill was dead. And there were no men out there waiting to rescue Anna like Alan Bates. Was he dead, too? Anna googled him on her phone. Yep, darling Alan was gone too.

Anna heard Ponytail start to sputter as the airline announced the flight would be delayed another hour. Anna grabbed her bag and purse and headed for the bar. "Anna, is that you?" she heard behind her. She turned and recognized a realtor she'd met a few conferences back.

"It's Karen," said the woman. Anna started to shake hands and the woman pulled her into a hug. She quickly gave Anna a condensed update on her life which involved a divorce and moving to a beach condo in San Diego. "It's wonderful. There are so many of us women of a certain age we call it Menopause Manor."

Anna asked her to join her for a drink but Karen said she was on her way to meet a client. They hugged again and Anna found a seat at the crowded bar.

Karen was younger than her, maybe in her mid-50s. Would Anna, in her late 60s, enjoy that life, living at the beach, hanging out with other single women? Moving somewhere nice would not be an obstacle. She had plenty of money. Thanks to the Bay Area's housing prices and fat commissions, Anna lived better than anyone in her family ever had. But did she want to be alone? What if the cancer came back? Who would be there when she got really old?

Yet, even if she stayed married, she really couldn't imagine Rick as a caregiver. He had his kind moments and he was remarkably patient with his mother. But taking care of a needy Anna, she wasn't sure. Of course, her friends would be around. They could create their own Menopause.. make that Medicare...Manor. But would they really do that? Jude was fine one moment, falling apart the next. Franny could well end up spending her sunset years with Jeffrey.

Now Anna was depressed and not looking forward to going home. Forget the Bloody Mary. She motioned to the bartender. "Double Stoli on the rocks."

CHAPTER THIRTY-TWO

JUDE HUGGED HERSELF IN her orange sweatshirt and admired the serene lake, glistening in the crisp September morning. Long years of drought had shrunk Lake Sonoma and exposed its scarred banks. But this year's rains had raised the reservoir and smoothed its raw edges, making it look more like its old self. Mother Nature's Botox, thought Jude.

Of course, it could just appear to be healthy. There were other things that can kill a lake besides drought. Pesticide run-off from the vineyards upstream plus any number of plant parasites that suck up the oxygen and starve the fish. A body of water, just like a human body, could look fine on the outside and be rotting underneath.

Geez, Jude, she chided herself. Can you give up the worst-case scenario for a couple of days? You're here to be with your friends. To have fun. No getting maudlin or crazy.

"Hey lady, how did you get here so fast?" Franny piled her camping gear next to Jude's and gave her a bear hug.

"Charlie drove me up," said Jude. "I said I was perfectly capable of getting here on my own but he worries about me driving with my bum foot."

"I agree with Charlie. But you made it. Feeling okay? Hey, you ditched the boot."

"Absolutely. I'm getting around pretty well. Katy brought me this very chic walking stick to help keep me balanced. And to fight off wild things." She waved it at Franny and pointed out the intricate sun and moon carvings and blue and orange stripes.

"Handsome, don't you think? Our Pomo sisters would approve."

They heard a boat motor and looked to see Anna aiming for the dock. She sounded *Lucia's* horn and hollered, "Let's go, women."

"Let me get the heavy stuff," Franny told Jude, dragging the coolers to the boat. "You just get yourself settled in."

They skimmed across the lake with no other boats in sight. "Wow, go cowgirl," said Franny, as the boat lurched and a grocery bag fell over. Franny grabbed runaway apples and wine bottles and Jude picked up a rolling lipstick.

The lake was theirs as was their favorite old campsite with the white Georgia O'Keefe tree still in the water. Anna cut the engine. Franny leaned over to feel the lake. "Warmer than the air. Still swimmable," she said, and jumped to shore to pull *Lucia* to the beach.

Anna declared, "My work is done" and sat back with a joint while Franny and Jude set up their tent. Anna said she would sleep out in the open on the boat. Had Janice come with them, had Janice been welcomed by Jude and Franny to accompany them, Anna would have invited her to unroll her sleeping bag on the deck and sleep beside her. They could have talked, listened for coyotes, gone to sleep with the moon in their faces.

It still pissed her off that her friends had been so against adding Janice, but Anna had promised herself not to bring it up again.

"Who belongs to this," asked Jude, holding up a lipstick. "Came rolling to my feet when you gunned the engine."

"Not mine, said Franny with a laugh. "I prefer going au naturel in the wild."

Anna studied the lipstick. "I'll take it." She pushed it into her jeans pocket and said, "Maybe we should get our lunch going."

Franny pointed to the cloudless sky. "Not me. I say it's time for the last skinny dip of the year." She started to peel off her clothes.

Jude watched her admiringly. "You still have the best boobs, Franny."

"Well thank you, pal. I'm happy to report that Jeffrey agrees with you."

"Boobs?" said Anna. "Do you really have to call them boobs? They're breasts for god's sake."

"Come on, Anna," said Jude as she pulled food from grocery

bags. "It's just a word. Oh, here's the crackers. I guess the cheese is all in the cooler."

"Yeah, and it's a word I happen to resent," said Anna. "They're breasts, damn it. Maybe I'm being over-sensitive but once you've fought as hard as I did, as hard as I still do, to keep mine alive and healthy, you don't call them some dopey name."

"Wow, Anna, no one's trying to be disrespectful here," said Franny.

"A boob is a word for a dopey person," said Anna, "and boob is a horrible word for breasts. I hate to hear it, especially from women."

Franny gave her a teasing look. "How about titties?"

"No. Not titties or tits or melons or hooters or jugs."

"Some very nice women call their breasts ta-tas," said Jude, trying to help. "That's not disrespectful."

"Nope," said Anna. "No. No. You guys are usually so PC. Why do you want to sound like some horny adolescent boy?"

"Well, okay then," said Franny. "Right now, however, I'm going to take my proud breasts for a swim. Come Louise. Come Thelma."

"We're just teasing, Anna," said Jude, muffling a laugh. She held out the box of crackers. "Eat something."

"No, I think I need a walk," said Anna, jumping to the beach.

"You said we should start lunch."

"I changed my mind."

Jude watched Anna march off down the beach, her back straight, probably still fuming. Jude thought she better never let on to Anna that Charlie sometimes called her breasts lamadams. That was the word, wasn't it? Sounded like the name of a fraternity. Lamadams would surely put Anna over the edge. She giggled and decided to have a beer. "Go ahead, friends," she said out loud. "Just leave me here to drink alone and fight off the wild pigs."

She looked at the bright yellow day. On the drive up, there were brilliant red and orange vineyards while at the lake the live oaks stayed green with a few brown leaves. But it smelled like fall, spicy and earthy with a tinge of leftover campfire smoke. The afternoon sun would bear down but then turn off quickly and the temperature would drop. Jude knew the night would come fast and cold.

She was contemplating another beer when she looked up to

see Anna walking rapidly toward the boat. Her face looked hot and red and she had taken off her jacket and was swatting it at the bushes like a machete.

"Okay, I've had it. I'm done. This is it. Do you hear me, Jude?" She shouted out to the lake, "Do you hear me, Franny?"

Anna's fierce voice scared Jude. Why was Anna yelling and was it Jude's fault? Had she missed something?

Franny seemed equally clueless. Her sleek seal head pushed up over the bow and she said, "What the hell is Anna yelling about?"

They stared at Anna who held up the lipstick tube. "This is not my lipstick. It was on the boat and I haven't been on the boat since last year with you guys. And look at this." She twisted open the lipstick. "It's coral. I hate coral. Have you ever seen me wear coral lipstick in my life?"

"I think it's actually more tangerine," said Franny, sending Anna and Jude a faint-hearted smile.

"It's not mine, Franny," Anna said. She clenched her fists and howled. "Damn you, Rick. Oh baby, it will never happen again," she said mockingly. "I only love you. I only want you."

"Anna, it doesn't necessarily have to mean that," said Jude. She tumbled her brain for other possibilities. "Maybe Rick brought his mother up fishing."

Anna barked a laugh. "Sure, Jude. Can you imagine Heather on any boat that wasn't a Viking Cruise?"

She pushed the lipstick back in her pocket. "No, this we label Evidence Number One."

Franny quickly pulled on shorts and a shirt. "Well, then, Anna, what do you want to do? We probably can't call him from here. There's not much cell service but we can try. You want to turn around and go home?"

Anna shook her head. "No, he's not going to fuck up our trip. This will wait. But I think I will get a little bit drunk. Damn him. I hate him."

"We hate him, too, sweetie," said Jude.

As the sun started to go down Franny assembled plates of smoked salmon, a jar of capers, two baguettes, a Greek salad and cold tarragon chicken. "Courtesy of Jeffrey. He wanted to make sure we ate well."

She passed plates around and then stopped. She threw her head back and laughed. "Oh, my gosh. You know what this is? This is part of our last meal menu. Jeffrey and I got into a discussion the other night about prisoners on death row getting to order their last meal."

Jude and Anna exchanged glances and started to eat.

"It was kind of a game. We said what we would want to eat for a last meal. And then Jeffrey, because he's Jeffrey and relates almost everything to a human rights issue, said he thought it was unfair to serve someone who is going to die their favorite food. Like it was a form of torture."

Anna rolled her eyes, "Here we go."

Jude stopped chewing and said, "Well, I'll play. For my last meal I would like some pasta carbonara at a Greenwich Village cafe with street musicians and one of those waiters who suddenly breaks into opera."

"That's good, Jude," said Franny.

Anna poured more wine and said, "Watch out what you say, Jude. You may see yourself in print."

"Huh? What do you mean?" said Jude.

"Our Franny could be taking notes."

"Go easy, Anna," said Franny, giving her a warning look. She turned to Jude. "What kind of wine would you want with that meal, Jude?"

"A nice Italian red. Doesn't go with carbonara necessarily, but who's going to get snooty at someone's last meal?" She grabbed the bottle. "Right now, I'll settle for this amusing white." She looked over at Anna who was glowering at Franny.

"What's going on?" asked Jude.

"Franny, tell her," said Anna. "Tell Jude what you want to write about."

Franny sighed. "Jude, I told Anna I was interested in writing about our obsession with dying. Okay, my obsession." She stammered, "You know, your obsession, too." Jude gave her a puzzled look.

"I thought I might have a character kind of like you, but not you, because this is going to be a novel, or it will be, if I ever write it. You know how I'm always talking about writing a book but never do it. Anyhow, you actually made me start thinking about it back when you were talking so much about getting what your mother had and how you were so worried about getting sick and dying."

"Franny darling," said Jude. "I was not worried about dying. However, I was, I am, worried about losing my brain and not dying. But I'm not sure you'd want me for your book."

Anna gave Franny a told-you-so look.

"Well, maybe it will be more about our generation getting old, facing mortality and all that," said Franny.

Jude looked amused. "Well, okay Franny, if you want to use me for research, go for it. Pick my brain." She smiled. "While there's something left to pick."

No one spoke for a while and then Franny moved over to Jude and put her arm around her. "Jude. I'm sorry. I won't do it. I mentioned it to Anna once and now I think she's right. It was a stupid idea. I don't want to write about dying. I don't want to think about any of us dying."

"Oh, you do, too, Franny," said Anna. "You're the one obsessed with the subject. Did she tell you, Jude, about going to a death cafe?"

Jude started to giggle. "Really? Is that where you go for your last meal?" She topped up her wine. "Actually, I've changed my mind."

Franny looked worried and Jude continued. "I think I'd rather have meatballs. With red sauce and spaghetti. No pasta-a-la-fancy. Just plain spaghetti and meatballs. I would spill some red sauce on my blouse and the waiter would bow and say, 'Signora, let me help.' And then he'd gently dab at my blouse with a towel and his hand would linger on my…" She looked at Anna. "On my breast. And then I could die."

Franny yelped. "Yes, yes. Bravo Jude."

Chapter Thirty-Three

Jude opened her eyes. It was dark, she was squished between two bodies and she needed to get out of the tent and pee but she hated to leave her warm and cozy nest. Snores came from Franny, burrowed deep in her sleeping bag, only her red curls showing. Anna was face down in her pillow. She'd been boozing it up last night. Maybe she'd passed out.

Jude thought back. When did Anna come into the tent? It must have been long after Jude and Franny had settled in. She remembered that Anna had unzipped the tent flap, said it was freezing on the boat and they needed to move over. Jude squeezed closer to Franny and Anna threw down her bag and crawled inside, eager to chat.

"Okay, I want to play the game," said Anna.

"Come on," groaned Franny. "We're sleeping."

Undaunted, Anna continued, "I want to play your last meal game. I've been thinking about it and I want tacos al pastor. Pulled pork. From this taco truck in Austin. Two, maybe three of them. With that amazing slaw they pile on top and three different salsas. And I'd want a margarita. No mix. Lots of fresh lime and top shelf tequila.

"Which salsa?" Franny muttered.

"The Habanero. Might as well go out with a fire in my belly."

"Very good," said Franny. "Now will you please shut up and let us sleep?"

Jude congratulated herself for being able to remember yesterday. It had been fun, all that talk about last meals. And, oh yeah, what was that about Franny writing a book and Jude being a part of it? Anna had been in a crappy mood because of Rick. But then she came into the tent all happy. And now here they were, snug as a bug in a rug, as Jude would tell Katy when she tucked her in on a cold night.

Even with Franny glommed to her side, Jude was able to slither out of her bag, find her flashlight and crawl out of the tent. Squatting a respectful distance from the tent she felt a jab of pain in her foot and chided herself for leaving her walking stick behind in the boat. Why did she do that? Did she want to show her friends she didn't need help? Stupid vanity.

There was a shiny sliver of moon above the flat lake. Her friends were missing a terrific view.

She heard a rustling behind her.

"Franny? Anna?"

Nobody answered. Jude pulled up her pajamas, stood and turned. It was a deer. A velvety big-eyed doe, one leg lifted in a ballet pose. They stared at each other. Jude smiled and whispered, "Hi there." The deer walked off, wiggled her fanny up the hill and turned to look at Jude. Then she went into the trees. Maybe it was Martha, come back to check in on her old camping pals. Why not? The natives believed this land was sacred so it was probably loaded with ghosts. If Jude waited maybe her mother would stop by for a visit. But which mother would she be, the sick one or the healthy one?

Jude started back to the tent as Franny stuck her head out and hissed, "Jude, where the hell have you been?"

"I had to pee."

"Well, I figured that, but you were gone a lot longer than it takes any woman, even our age, to pee."

"Oh, Franny, you worry too much."

Jude crawled back into her sleeping bag and the next thing it was morning and she heard Franny and Anna outside the tent discussing the weather. "I'd say our blue skies are gone," said Franny. "It could clear up and I really want to go for another swim. But if it's going to be cool and overcast maybe we should pack up early and skip tonight."

"We're not going anywhere," said Anna. "We said we were

coming here for two nights and we are."

Jude shouted, "I vote we stay." She was feeling lighter, freer here than she did at home. She rolled over in her bag and fell back to sleep.

By mid-afternoon Franny announced the water warm enough to swim and Anna, who had spent the morning in the boat, saying she didn't feel like talking, especially about Rick, agreed it was time to motor over to the cove. As they churned across the lake, Franny slyly looked over at Jude. She put two fingers to her mouth like she was inhaling a joint, signaling that their captain might be a little stoned.

When they got to the cove Anna backed in and Franny, stripped down to T-shirt and underpants, tied the stern line to a branch.

"Okay, swim baby," said Anna, reaching behind to the cooler. "Is it wine time, Jude?"

"Oh, let's wait until we get back," said Jude. She moved up to the bow to dangle her legs in the water and looked up at the weak sun and round hills. "Now this is living. What more could you want?"

"Right," said Anna, a little bitterly, taking her silver tin from her jacket pocket and lighting up. She took a couple of puffs, stubbed it out and put it back in the tin. "Do you think I should cut my hair? Get some bangs."

"What? No, I like your long hair," said Jude. "You're one of the few women our age who can wear it like that. It's full, it's healthy. It's Anna hair."

"But don't you think it makes me look old? Don't you ever worry about that?"

"Looking old?" Jude laughed, patting her belly. "Sure, who doesn't? But I can't say it's at the top of my current worry list."

"Well maybe it doesn't matter if you have a man like Charlie who will love you forever just the way you are."

"I'm not so sure of that," said Jude.

They watched Franny power herself out of the cove toward the middle of the lake, doing a strong and steady free style, then flipping into a graceful back stroke. She looked back at the boat and hollered, "Hoo-hah."

"Look how elegantly she does that," said Jude. "How come I can't swim like that?" She looked over at Anna. "Earth to Anna, are you here?"

"Oh, sure. Just thinking," said Anna.

Then it happened, so fast. Franny swam back to the boat and went to untie the rope. Anna started the ignition and put the boat in idle and said, "Hurry it up, Franny. Jude said we can't drink until we get back to camp."

Franny tossed the rope to Jude who bent over the side of the boat to give Franny a hand up as Franny said, "Wait a minute." She slipped back into the water. "Let me look. I think the prop could be stuck on something."

Anna didn't hear Franny. Just as Jude yelled, "Hold it, Anna," the boat slowly began to move. But in reverse.

Jude watched Franny's eyes grow huge and her mouth open into a scream. Later Jude wondered if Franny had actually made a noise or if it was Jude who had screamed.

Anna looked back and cried, "Oh no, oh no." She put the boat in neutral, turned off the motor as Jude jumped into the water and grabbed Franny. The water turned red.

Anna and Jude pulled Franny into the boat. Franny's leg was gushing blood. "Oh God, oh shit," cried Franny, panting and shuddering. "We've got to get out of here." Jude grabbed a towel which was quickly soaked with Franny's blood. Anna grabbed another towel.

"Quick, Anna," said Jude, "We need to stop the bleeding." Anna was stumbling and crying, "I'm sorry. I'm so sorry, Franny." Jude looked around the boat and found a bungee cord in a side pocket. She tied it above the long deep slash the boat's propeller had carved into Franny's tanned muscled thigh. Jude pulled the cooler over and propped Franny's leg on it.

"Okay, Anna, your job is to keep her leg elevated and the cord tight. I'll drive."

"No, you can't, Jude. You don't know how," protested Anna, moving toward the driver's seat. Jude pushed her aside. "Get back there. I'm driving the damn boat. You take care of Franny."

"I think she's passing out," cried Anna.

"Talk to her. Just keep talking to her."

Jude turned the key, pushed the throttle forward and the boat, thank you *Lucia*, began to move. "Do you have your phone?" Jude shouted at Anna. "See if you can get a signal and call 911."

"Nothing. No. Yes, yes. I've got it. I'm calling," Anna shouted back.

"Please, please, please," Jude said, pointing them toward the marina, making jerky swaths across the lake as Jude tried to master the steering. She found the black button that was the horn and *Lucia* let out a weak honk as they crossed the empty lake. There was no other boat around, no water skiers, no jet ski cowboys, no rescuers in sight. She kept honking.

They rounded the tree-lined shore and Jude saw the marina buildings ahead. "Thank you, thank you," she said. A figure on the dock was waving a hat at them.

"Ease back on the throttle," Anna said, her voice now calm and encouraging. "You need to start slowing down."

Jude pulled back on the throttle and the boat obeyed. "Good job, Jude," said Anna, cushioning Franny as Jude made an inelegant direct hit on the dock where Pearl, the marina store clerk who called everyone "Honey" and sold them a camping pass and red licorice the morning before, was waiting. She shouted, "Throw me the line."

"What? Where is the goddamn line?" yelled Jude.

Pearl pointed to the rope on the bow and Jude stood up, leaned over the steering wheel and grabbed the rope. She tossed it to Pearl who cinched *Lucia* to a cleat on the dock just as the stern started to drift out.

"Grab this, too," Anna yelled and pointed the handle of Jude's walking stick at Pearl who pulled them in. They heard an ambulance siren.

The two EMTs strapped a pneumatic tourniquet, which looked like a big white Styrofoam balloon, on Franny's leg and carried her up the boat ramp in a gurney. Anna and Jude walked on either side of the stretcher.

"You'll be okay now," said Jude. Franny nodded, eyes and nose running, as the EMTs put her in the back of the ambulance.

While one EMT called ahead to the hospital the other said to

Jude, "You seem to be the one in charge. Tell me who we have here." Jude started rattling off Franny's vital information, when the EMT stopped her. "Name, address, age, enough. We've got to go. See you at the hospital. Healdsburg General."

He turned back. "Just want you both to know that tourniquet probably saved your friend's life. Bungee cord. Good choice. And you kept your heads."

The ambulance started up. Jude reached for Anna's hand as it drove away.

Chapter Thirty-Four

In Anna's nightmare it happened slowly. She looked down and watched her hand put the boat in gear and then pull the lever in reverse. In her nightmare the lake turned to blood and the motor's knives filleted Franny into many pieces. In her nightmare she heard Franny cry "Oh God, no," an alarm that wrapped around the lake and ricocheted off the steep hills. And then Anna, too, would scream, and when she woke up her throat was raw.

After the accident Anna sent flowers to Franny's hospital room but it took her days to walk into her front yard and collect a bunch of Naked Ladies to deliver in person.

As she rode up in the elevator Anna berated herself. How could she have done such a thing? She had never hurt anyone in her life. She had never been in a school yard fight or spanked her little boy or slapped her unfaithful louse of a husband.

She might have blamed her sloppy drunken stoned state that day on Rick and the woman with the coral lips. She might have blamed the tequila and the wine and the pot. But there was no way to rationalize the reckless stupid act that almost killed her friend. Anna wished for her old catechism priest to tell her what to do to be forgiven. Alone, she could not come up with enough penance.

Hoping that Franny would be asleep and she could scribble a note with the flowers and leave, Anna took a breath and opened the door to Franny's room.

"Oh good, it's you," said Franny, waving her in.

Clutching the floppy tall pink bouquet to her chest, Anna

started sobbing. "Franny, I am so sorry. So very, very sorry."

Franny held out her hand. "I know that you are, Anna." She pointed to her full-length leg cast, hoisted up in a sling, bare foot sticking out. "Look, they fixed me all up. And one of the nurses even painted my toenails."

Wiping her nose and wet face on her sleeve Anna awkwardly bent over Franny to twist herself into a hug. "I don't know how you'll ever forgive me. I can't bear that I did this to you."

"I've already forgiven you, Anna," said Franny, patting her on the back. "Well, almost. I'm not that much of a saint. But we're too old to find new best friends. And we've got to stop meeting in hospitals."

Franny drew back and put her hands together. "How about our Jude? What a super woman."

"I know," said Anna. "It was like the old Jude coming to our rescue."

Anna was dry-eyed and composed the night she confronted Rick. They were on the couch watching the news, Rick with a beer and Anna a pot of tea when she picked up the remote and silenced the TV.

"Hey, what are you doing?" said Rick.

"We need to talk," said Anna, moving to a chair across from the couch. "When we were up at the lake we found a lipstick in the boat."

"Lipstick? So? Whose lipstick?"

"You tell me, Rick. Wasn't mine. Who have you been taking out in the boat?"

Rick put his head back and sighed, "Aww Anna, what are you talking about?"

"You're going to tell me that you haven't been seeing someone?" Anna said, surprising herself that she didn't sound at all angry. She actually felt relaxed. She'd spent her rage at the lake, went a little crazy and practically killed Franny. Now she wanted this over. No need for fireworks. She might have liked to smash a pie in his face like Meryl Streep did to Jack Nicholson in *Heartburn*, but that wasn't her style. She and Rick didn't fight with much passion, hadn't in fact done anything with much passion for some time.

"Please, Rick, don't lie to me."

He rubbed his forehead. "Okay. I won't. But it was just a stupid fling. It's long over."

Anna fiddled with the tea bag, smiling at the label. Tension Tamer. She only half-listened as Rick went on. She'd heard it before.

"I don't know why I did it. I don't want her. I want you. Only you." He started to get up and go to her but she put out her hand to stop him.

"But, I don't want you, Rick," she said. "And I'm not convinced you really do want me. What I know is I don't want to do this anymore. I don't want to do us anymore. It makes me too sad." She noticed how clear and calm her voice sounded as she said out loud what she'd been thinking for some time. "I feel stuck. I want something different. I don't want to die and have people say, she sold a lot of houses and made a lot of money but she wasn't very happy. I need more. I think we both do."

"So, what are you saying," he said. "You want me to leave?"

Anna studied her husband. He was a good-looking man, not much different in appearance than when they fell in love, plus soft belly and gray beard. He was not an awful person, and right now he looked bewildered. She thought he was probably feeling lost and she kind of felt sorry for him. She was pissed at him but she didn't hate him. She imagined they could eventually turn into one of those divorced couples who stay cordial, maybe even hug when they ran into each other at Safeway.

"I've thought about it," she said. "We don't need to rush into this. But maybe you could go stay with your friend Steve for a while. He has that studio he uses for an Airbnb. Eventually I can buy you out of the house. I had a pretty good year."

"But wait a damn minute, Anna," said Rick. He twisted his hands. "You're going too fast. We could work this out. We've been together so long. We can't quit now."

Anna smiled and sipped her tea. "We worked it out once before, Rick. And now it's happened again. And probably will again."

He stared at her and said nothing as she continued. "And you're right. We've been together a long time and we are getting older. That's exactly why I want to quit now."

"Well," he stammered, "what am I supposed to do about my mother? What am I going to tell her?"

"Oh, Heather and I have already talked," said Anna. "She can stay."

"You told her? But you don't even like my mother."

"Obviously, you haven't been paying attention. Heather and I have been getting along pretty well. In fact, at this moment I'd rather live with her than you."

Five Years Later

Jude took off her glasses, smiled at the audience and closed Franny's book, *California Dying*. As hoped, the silver-haired crowd on the cruise ship looked eager to find out more.

"Many of you told me that you've already read the book and now I've told you my friends' and my story. You're probably all thinking, well, then what?

"Obviously I decided not to kill myself. My brain came awake that terrifying afternoon at the lake five years ago and I knew exactly what to do. It was like the fog, the confusion, cleared and I simply acted. And after that I decided, *okay Jude*, looks like your addled brain is still working."

Pushing her hair from her forehead, Jude continued, "Imagine. All those times I spent second guessing every little thing I did and said. Consumed by fear. Making myself crazy, for God's sake. And suddenly the old me, the old Jude stepped in and took over."

She opened a bottle of water, cleared her throat and took a sip. "Dry mouth. Always happens when I speak. Anyhow, I tell you, it was good to have me back.

"I went to see Franny in the hospital after the accident. That was one big bite the propeller dug out of our Franny's leg. A lot of flesh and a chunk of bone. It took some complicated surgery to put her leg back together. Franny walked with a limp after that.

"I went into her room and she patted the bed for me to sit. I did and she took my hand. She was on pain pills so her voice was a little groggy. 'Jude, my darling,' she kind of slurred, 'I don't think you need to kill yourself anymore.' Well, I said to her, I hope that doesn't ruin your book on dying. Franny said that was okay because she hadn't written the ending yet."

Jude pointed to the stack of books next to the podium. *California Dying* by Franny Gordon. "This is what she finally ended up with. The book isn't just about me. I might have inspired it and I am kind of the focus, but Franny ended up interviewing all types of people. About getting older and worrying about what's going to get you in the end. We started calling her the Queen of Death.

"Franny's book helped open up the conversation, even though you and I know that most people would still rather talk about the weather or their cute new shoes than acknowledge their mortality.

"So, now I give speeches and help sell her book, which I'm happy to say is in its second printing. It landed me on this big floating hotel. With how many pools and elevators? Gosh, there must be a mojito bar everywhere you turn."

The audience laughed. A man in a pink shirt held up his drink glass and shouted, "Salud."

Jude waved her water bottle at him and laughed. "Personally, I don't drink alcohol anymore. But I do appreciate you having a good time. I like these senior cruises especially when they ask speakers like me to get on board." Jude did a curtsy. "I appreciate folks who know how to have fun, and are also willing to talk about some of the dark stuff.

"Speaking of which, back to my Alzheimer nightmare. Turns out I didn't have my mother's disease and as far as I know I still don't." She thumped her knuckles on the podium. "Sadly, my tough cousin, Betty the cop, she got it. Shitty disease. Makes no sense who it goes after."

Spotting a frowning woman wrapped in green pashmina, Jude said, "You want to ask me the question, right?"

The woman looked around and stood up. "Well yes, Jude, from what I read in the book and what you've told us about your fear of dementia, can you catch us up? What was actually wrong with you?"

Jude nodded. "I know, it sure sounded like I was losing my marbles. Instead, simply put, it was a mixture of alcohol and deep depression, plus this immobilizing dread that I may lose my mind. My fear put me in a lonely place. It cut me off not only from my friends and family but myself. I was drinking a whole lot more than anyone, including me, realized. It was the only way I could get my brain to stop catastrophizing."

"Amen," said a woman in the back, bobbing her sunhat in agreement.

Pointing from the podium, Jude called to the woman, "You, too, I see."

The woman stood up and said, "Well, yes. I know all about worry-mind. Now I'm in a group for anxiety. Have you tried meditation?"

"Tried it all," said Jude, getting sympathetic nods from several in the audience. "Therapist, support group, alcohol program. All helps. But I've got another thing."

She dug around in her jacket pocket and held up a small white rock. "When I start going down the rabbit hole—I'm still a big catastrophizer—I pull out this little stone. Anna gave it to me as a souvenir from the lake and a reminder to have courage."

Jude gave the stone a little rub and said, "Works better than a bottle of Sauvignon Blanc."

She sipped more water and sighed. "Before you ask about the others, I want to talk about Charlie, my sweet man. It's amazing how much a couple can hide from one another. You think you know all about a man. Like how he always sleeps in his socks and his first love was his next-door neighbor. But then, on some major issue, you can be absolutely clueless.

"I blamed myself for some of this. Charlie was hiding something from me, too. I was so desperate to act like I was perfectly fine I didn't really pay much attention to anyone else. Charlie suspected he had a bad heart and I should have wondered when he didn't go on his annual fishing trip to the High Sierra. Turned out he was afraid the altitude would kill him. Didn't want to worry anyone, he said later. Sound familiar?

"Finally, Katy noticed her dad kept running out of breath and got him to see a doctor. They put in a pacemaker that gave Charlie a couple more years. A chance for us to come clean with each other." Jude's voice cracked. "To love each other. To cuddle each other. We'd sit in the garden and listen to ballgames on the radio. Took the ferry over to San Francisco for one game.

"He told me he'd never worried that I was becoming like my mom. He said he thought I was just getting a little flakey and that maybe someday he'd have to take away my car keys, but we'd be okay.

"Charlie died at home. Just like a lot of people in Franny's book. He got to be in our living room and look at the finches and scold me for not pruning the roses his way. Hospice was there and Katy and Franny and Anna, plus Charlie's priest and some of the home funeral people Franny met researching her book.

"He even agreed to the Threshold Choir coming over to sing. You know them? They sing at the bedsides of ill and dying people. Whatever you want to hear. Charlie asked for his favorite Leonard Cohen. *Hallelujah*, what else? And a couple of Willie Nelson songs. Charlie grinned the whole time. Even his stuffy priest declared it a spiritual experience."

A hand shot up and a woman with a Chihuahua said, "I'm so sorry about Charlie. I lost my husband, too"

"Thank you, it's a rough one, but let's chain gears. Remember Anna? Anna got a divorce. Then she started spending every minute with her neighbor Janice. Soon they became a couple and not long after Rick moved out, Janice moved in. Heather, Anna's mother-in-law, continued to live there, too. Heather said it reminded her of her Alpha Gamma Delta days.

"Heather got a lousy cancer which really annoyed her. She kept saying she was supposed to drop dead of a heart attack. The cancer was pretty ruthless but before it got too bad Heather decided to end it.

"Unfortunately, the California aid in dying law wasn't going to work for Heather. She couldn't get doctors to agree she had less than six months to live and so she went ahead on her own. Anna did Heather's hair in an upsweep, helped her put on a sky-blue silk gown that Heather said her late husband especially liked, then Heather gave a queenly wave and drank her Seconal cocktail. She went so peacefully. I'm not sure where she got the stuff. Heather had contacts.

"You see, what I've been giving you is a kind of short-hand epilogue. That's in honor of our Franny. She loved epilogues. She always wanted to go beyond the last chapter. So, let me tell you about Franny.

"This book of hers was a big hit and she finally got to leave her job. She and Jeffrey went on book tours together, Jeffrey sticking fast to his belief against assisted dying. He said no one should be able to kill themselves with state approval. Franny disagreed. Sometimes the two of them would do a James Carville-Mary Matalin thing, bickering back and forth on stage. Jeffrey in his wheelchair, Franny on her cane."

Jude leaned both elbows on the podium, rubbed her eyes and exhaled loudly. "It was briefly on the news. Oh gosh, this is always so hard to say. Franny and Jeffrey died."

Gasps came from the crowd. "I know, it just seems so wrong. They were flying home after a trip to Ireland and were on that plane that went down over Greenland."

She slumped and said, "Sorry. I still can't believe that Franny is dead. Losing an old friend feels like an abandonment. I know some of you have been through this. It's hell, isn't it?"

Many in the audience nodded.

"At the same time, you have to be grateful you had each other. Sometimes when Anna and I get together we watch the movie *Evening*. It was a book by Susan Minot and in the movie Vanessa Redgrave and Meryl Streep have been best friends since they were young and now they're old and one is dying and they tell each other stories. To remember who they were. That's one of the wonders of old friends. They help recall details that make you realize a lot of life has been really good. It's like Anna says, friends are like medicine. They fix you up."

Jude tilted her head and grinned. "Or maybe Franny said that. Or maybe I did.

"Anyhow, my fellow voyagers, that's how I'll end this. If you want books, I'm selling them. If you want more answers, meet me in the bar. You can buy me a Nojito. It's a mojito without the kick."

The audience stood and applauded. The woman in the pashmina bowed down toward Jude. The guy in pink gave her a thumbs-up. After the book sales, Jude walked out of the room onto the deck and leaned on a railing. Later she'd text Anna and tell her how it went. But first she wanted to look up at the sky, loaded with stars, and underneath, feel the sea rushing toward her.

Acknowledgments

My characters are all fictional though many of the anecdotes, stories and better lines came from the recollections of friends and family. Nothing like hanging out with tale-telling people to inspire a writer with a notebook in her pocket.

I'm grateful to my writing group, book club, women's group and all those old friends and early readers who kept me writing and laughing in sweet and hard times. Special thanks to daughter/writer Samantha Rose for her patience and careful editing.

Made in the USA
San Bernardino, CA
08 July 2019